CAT IN CHARGE

CANDY RAE

AND

SAMSON THE CAT

CAT IN CHARGE

This book is a work of fiction. All characters in this publication are fictitious and any resemblance to real persons, living or dead, is purely coincidental.

Cover Image and Artwork by Harri Crawford

Book interior by Candy Rae with help from Creativindie Design.

First Edition: September 2017

ISBN-13: 978-1976079634

ISBN-10: 1976079632

'*Cat in Charge*' is dedicated to all cats, big and small, but especially one, in remembrance of a beautiful and feisty, black and white cat called Delilah, the sister of Samson.

Also, we wish to say great big thank you to our readers, Fiona, Nancy, James, Daniel, Mae, Whitepaw, Blackpaw and Toots.

BOOKS BY CANDY RAE

PLANET WOLF SERIES

(1) WOLVES AND WAR

(2) CONFLICT AND COURAGE

(3) HOMAGE AND HONOUR

(4) DRAGONS AND DESTINY

(5) VALOUR AND VICTORY

(6) AMBITION AND ALAVIDHA

(THE PREQUELS) PAWS AND PLANETS

(SHORT STORIES) TALES AND TAILS

DRAGON WULF SERIES

(1) JOURNEY AND JEOPARDY

(2) GOSSAMER AND GRASS

(3) FLAMES AND FREEDOM

T'QUEL MAGIC TRILOGY

(1) EPHEMERAL BOUNDARY

(2) ENDURING BARRIER

(3) ETERNAL BULWARK

KILL BY CURE

CAT AT CHRISTMAS

INTRODUCTION

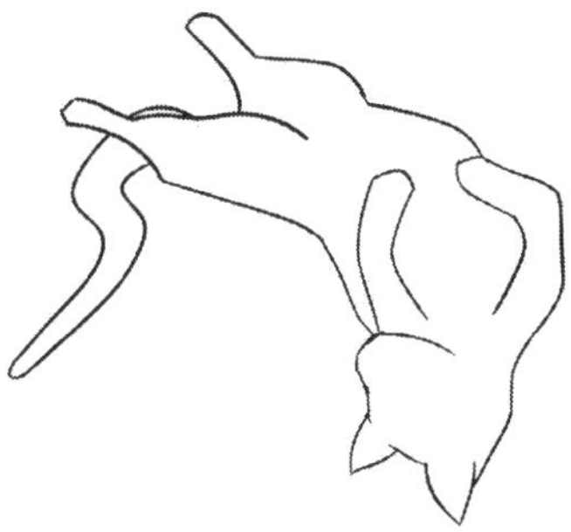

Just so you know, the reason why my name, Samson the Cat, is not on the cover as *the* writer of this book is because in this world we live in, we cats can't set up internet accounts or enter into publishing. That is the *one and only* reason. I don't want to get into an argument about what cats are capable of and what they are not. I *am* the author. Deal wif it.

In addition to this, and before we begin, I need to make a few points.

The idea that cats can't read and write is ridiculous. It is a rumour started by a dog-inspired conspiracy a long time ago when dogs must have been cleverer than they are now.

I know this for a fact.

What do you fink we are doing when you leave your computer and come back to see us lying in front of, or on, the keyboard?

Why do you fink we sit on your lap when you are reading?

What really happens when you are *encouraged* to put down your newspaper so you can tickle us?

Why is it that every time you come back to your armchair to read you find us sitting on it, paper or book by our side?

We are getting an education, that's what we are doing.

Back to the writing problem …

The reason is everyfing to do wif anatomy. What is specifically unfortunate is my lack of opposable thumbs. The tapping of the keys on keyboards takes a lot of time and is full of errors. My human however, wif a lot of help from me, is able to decipher what letters make up words and which do not.

So, I suppose writing is not so much of a problem after all.

Also, the screen is a huge distraction. I can concentrate on the keyboard, type the word, but when I look at the screen to check the spelling it is *so* interesting, I often forget what I have been doing.

If I try to type and screen watch at the same time, disaster!

My paw goes straight to the word on the screen and would you know it? As I press forward to see better, lots more letters appear!

It's a cat fing and I know that those perfidious mice and birds have somefing to do wif it.

However, my human and I are working very well together on this writing fing. I direct and human obeys. I find the best place to oversee is sitting along human shoulders against back of chair. This leaves paws free to correct.

This correction of errors might not be a simple swat. It means me using claws on its paws to indicate when human has made a mistake. This happens more often than you would fink.

And regarding those perfidious mice; there *must* be a conspiracy. There just has to be.

This conspiracy is not between my human and the mice. My human is terrified of the little fings wif tails that scurry along the ground. I can't understand it, but … therein lies the difference between cats and humans.

They are frightened of such silly fings.

Therefore …

Someone inside the house must become the fearless leader.

Dogs? Certainly not! I fink their bravery is questionable and a great big bluff. May I also say that we all know that a great big bluff is the same fing as a great big lie? Dogs are also really, really stupid. I will talk more about this stupidity later, but I ask you, what animal in its right mind would roll around in fox poop?

As the only ones capable of commanding a house, we cats must step in.

This is why we cats are in charge.

This is why *I* am in charge.

CHAPTER 1

MUM

To say a cat doesn't remember everyfing is stupid!

We remember *everyfing*. Every good deed, every slight, *everybody*.

I remember when I was very small I couldn't see anyfing. Of course this was long before my human took me to its house and I learned that kittens are born wif their eyes shut. I fink we will say it was the eyes.

The same went for the hearing bit. I can't remember what came first, the hearing or the sight but it must have been at around the same time.

All my siblings were blind too but Mum was there, wif delicious milk, a warm body and a rough tongue.

There was also some spiky stuff. Straw, I fink.

I never knew my father. Actually, I'm not sure Mum did either. Cats don't do the marriage fing. This is normal. Cats may fight, but kittens are abundant. She was a farm cat so knew all about it.

Dad was somefing 'they' called 'feral'. 'They' is a word we can use interchangeably wif 'humans' and 'cats' and other animals.

It wasn't until much later, when I taught myself to read and looked it up the dictionary that I learned what 'feral' meant.

It doesn't matter.

A cat is what a cat is and Mum brought us all up just right.

When my eyes opened there was a whole new world to explore but I was always moving around under Mum's watchful eye.

The 'opening of the eyes' is a very important day for a cat. I remember Mum licked me very thoroughly that morning. The extra licks were her gift to me on that special day, affection by tongue.

I'm an honest cat so have to admit that the affectionate licks helped me to stay calm. The brightness of the light was scary in the beginning.

A few days after this I began to hear. That was spooky too but I soon got used to it.

Mum was amazing.

The barn was absolutely gigantic and full of the most wonderful fings of fun.

There were huge spiders crawling up and down long transparent ropes.

There were little mice and big mice scurrying around the straw. Mum taught us to listen for movement under the hay and straw and the sounds of their paw steps. Thrilling!

And then there were the birds. They were better than the

mice.

Mum explained that birds are tricky to catch because they can fly away. This, she said, made catching a bird far more interesting and satisfying.

She told us to watch and listen.

She showed us all what to do when the time came for us all to start hunting.

All? I hear you ask.

There were five of us.

I fink there might have been six of us at the beginning; at least I remember a sense that there was another whom I never saw, but he or she must have left us before the opening of the eyes.

Anyway, we were five. Mum had a special name for each of us.

It was a cat name, and not at all the same kind of name a human might use.

My human calls me 'Samson' or 'Sammy'.

Incidentally, it also uses 'clever boy', 'genius', 'handsome' and 'wonderful'.

Mum's 'name' for me was 'Mleeip'. It means, in cat, little one. One of my sisters was called 'Myup' and the other 'Mrru', and my two brothers 'Meiu' and "Mrrup'.

Together we learned how to spot, to stalk and to hunt, practicing on each other at first then trying out our skills (or lack of them) on the occasional mouse that ventured too close.

If we missed, which was most of the time, Mum jumped in to help. She was a very good hunter.

The man farmer called her 'a great mouser'. Mum told us this meant she got all the best tidbits when the lady farmer was disposing of scraps such as bits of end cuts of a meat called beef. This didn't concern us very much when she told us because we loved her milk and anyfing else we only licked at or nibbled.

One day, when we went to the milk bank to get our morning snack of creamy milk, Mum pushed us away.

She told us we had to start eating food like the adult cats ate.

To start us off she brought a mouse over and laid it down in front of us, holding it by the tail.

This was very exciting. It was squeaking, very high. The hairs inside my ears were prickling.

I felt my tail twitching and Mum told me to keep it still. Mice are very sensitive to twitching tails.

The waiting was awful but just as we thought we couldn't bear the suspense any longer, she killed it.

She divided the mouse up between us and told us to start eating.

It was very tasty.

Mum explained about the bones and said we should lick round them in the beginning. One day our teeth would be big and strong enough to crunch the biggest bone but not yet.

It was not long after that first fresh meat meal when I met my first rat.

Met, not saw.

Mum had explained all about rats as soon as we could see. Rats are a danger to kittens because they fink kittens are prey.

Mice squeak but rats hiss, squeak and chatter.

We had heard them scuttling around, and each time we did we would call the alarm. Mum always came and chased it away.

However, that day she must have been further away.

I pushed through some straw and came face-to-face wif the nasty fing.

It was almost as big as me!

I miaowed.

Mum didn't come, I fink she was hunting outside somewhere, but my sister Myup arrived instead.

My sister was wonderful. She was bigger and stronger and braver than me, at least when we were small.

Actually, if I'm honest, I fink she was my half sister, because she was different in temperament and looks. Mum wasn't exactly, in terms a human might understand, married, so I'm positive that, in hindsight, I've hit the mark right on the mouse's head.

Black was our predominant colour, and as it is well known that black cats are the handsomest, I am very pleased about this. I am black from the end of my tail to the tippety-top of my ears except for a little tuft of white along my side. Myup though, she was black and white. Humans called her a 'tuxedo'. I've never understood this. I've seen pictures of tuxedos and they looked nofing like Myup.

Her coat was thin and shiny whereas mine is as thick as a shaggy rug; a good fing on a farm where a cat's indoors is a draughty barn. I have always felt a thick coat is useful, especially during the winter when I want to stay outside all night. Of course, there is a downside - the brush and the comb.

As the days and nights passed we five grew bigger. We no longer drank milk but ate meat, raw and new killed.

I hit a snag during these days. Actually, it was more than a snag; it was life threatening. I was the smallest and my co-ordination was not good at all. The others got more to eat than I did and while Mum brought me somefing from time to time, there was not much meat on my bones. I grew thinner and my coat became dirty and unkempt because I was so tired all the time.

One day the man farmer came to choose which two cats would remain on the farm and which three were to be sold on.

I've never really understood the concept of money so when it said ten pounds for Myup and Meiu and seven for me I didn't understand. However. I know now that it couldn't have thought much of me. If I could go back to that farm today, I might be persuaded to scratch its eyes out.

I've always felt this was an odd turn of phrase, I mean, sold on to what?

Mrru and Mrrup were staying on the farm. They were the best hunters, having already caught a mouse each but Myup was just as good. Perhaps the man farmer thought she was too delicate for the rough and tumble of farm life.

So, off the three of us went, into a cage, to await our fate.

Mum came to visit us at the cage and told us what was happening. It was always so, she explained, and we were not to worry. All would be well.

A lady human came and looked at us. To my shame, I was scared and sat shaking at the back of the cage. Myup tried to shelter me but Meiu went forward and pressed his nose against the mesh.

The lady human chose him, and once he was in a grey plastic box wif mesh at one end I saw the lady human give him chicken! Real chicken like the scraps the lady farmer sometimes threw out, to the great delight of all the farm cats.

I never saw Meiu again.

I learned a lot in that moment but the most important lesson was that humans are here to provide nice fings for cats.

The next day (or at least I fink it was the next day; my sense of time is a bit imprecise), another lady human arrived at the farm. It was carrying a box very like the box the last lady human had been carrying.

I was interested at the prospect of chicken but still scared. Myup though, she went straight up to it and rubbed herself against the mesh. Show-off.

Again I, to my shame, cowered at the back, hoping to remain unnoticed.

However, it appeared the lady human had other ideas. I heard it talking to the man farmer and it handed over somefing that rustled and clinked.

My nose twitched but it didn't sound like chicken being unwrapped so I stayed right where I was.

The man farmer opened the door and thrust its hand inside to grab Myup. She didn't like the suddenness of it and hissed.

I thought that might be the end of it but the lady human appeared unfazed by this show of bad manners. It opened the door of the box and the man farmer shoved Myup inside.

I decided to remain as still as I possibly could. I was under the misguided misapprehension that if I remained still and quiet, they would not see me. I was wrong. I was as wrong as wrong can be. The man farmer pushed its arm in and grabbed me.

I went limp.

I thought at the time that if I pretended to be asleep the hands would go away.

Myup sent me a cheerful chirrup and I opened one eye but I was being pushed into the box so I shut it again. She was much braver than me.

The lady human and the man farmer talked a little more then began walking away from the barn.

Mum was watching from a fence a short distance away. She told us to be brave and to remember to be a cat and not a lapdog.

This didn't mean anyfing to my sister or me at the time but I understand what she meant now. It was the best piece of advice anyone has given me.

Thank you Mum.

CHAPTER 2

HOUSE

We travelled in a motorcar. Myup, who had been so brave up until now began to tremble so much I could hear her teeth rattling. I wet the fluffy fing I was lying on, (I know now it was a blanket). The lady human had believed it was being kind when it had placed it there but Myup and me would have much preferred a bundle of straw. Straw soaks up necessaries very well, smells nice and would have reminded us of home, sort of comforting. As it was, the peculiar scent off the blanket produced the exact opposite effect from what was intended.

I disgraced myself again not long after the wetting of the blanket, if I remember correctly. Actually I do remember. Being sick has no effect on a cat's ability to forget nofing.

As we were bumping along the lady human began to sniff.

I looked at Myup and she looked at me.

Would the lady human notice?

I'm sure it did but it was very polite about it, almost catlike. It didn't mention it at all.

The motorcar stopped at last.

I looked at Myup.

She looked as scared as I felt but we had come to an understanding during the journey. We weren't going to show the lady human how scared we were.

We were cats and cats never show fear.

It's the first rule.

Never show fear, in spite of, or because of how we are feeling inside.

This might be a good time to talk about the language of cat.

It must be understood that when we miaow, even if another cat is around, we are not actually having a long and convoluted conversation wif them. As a kitten will miaow when wanting the attention of Mum, so will we when we are demanding attention from you. Note the change in the verb; 'want' to 'demand'. It is very important.

This is because we want you to believe we are still kittens and unable to catch our own food. This ploy has been very successful through the ages. The faster and louder the miaow is, the more urgent the demand is.

Some humans (they call themselves animal psychologists and claim to be able to understand cats - how utterly ridiculous is that?) say that a deeper miaow means that we are uncomfortable or in pain.

Believe me, if the pain got so bad that we had to tell a

human (and it would have to be very bad) you'd know about it. Our pain complaints certainly wouldn't be a simple plaintive and loud miaow. There would be pain inflicted.

It will also interest you to know that there are many variations in the spelling of miaow. There are miaow, miaow, miau, mew and probably others. I like 'miaow' best so that is the one I will use. On the cat wide web, there is a on-going discussion regarding spelling issues. I may have contributed a few comments of my own.

The main problem is the 't-h' and the 'f' fing. One side of the garden fence wants one and the other side wants the other. Personally, I fink we should go wif the 'f' and be done wif it. However, cats love an argument and I am no exception.

Most humans like to hear us purr. It happens most often when we decide to sleep on a human's lap or push in beside it. We can't help but purr when we are warm, well fed, and comfortable.

Petting is also a good fing but only when we want the pettings. All humans must understand that we only want to be petted when we want to be petted. This is a rule and any infringements to this rule will always be punished.

These pesky animal psychologists also say purring is hypnotic. I would like to ask to whom? Purring does not send me into a trance, despite the fact it may seem like I am in one. Please also remember that a purr does not always mean that all is well. I can purr wif my ears flat quite well and this will not bode well for the human.

There is also the language of birds.

We learn about this first from Mum and then from other

cats. Kittens use these to get attention. Mums use it for the same reason. However, the language of birds is spoken when we are happy and thrilled about somefing. This happens often when we are watching birds, hence the name for the chirrups, cheeps and quavers that a human hears.

Talking of birds and windows, I always fink of birds when I fink of windows and vice versa; there is another sound we make, a sound closely affiliated to the language of birds. It's a noise like a human cutting vegetables but much faster and is made by hitting our teeth together very fast. I get very excited when I see birds outside the window especially if they fly on to the window ledge to taunt me.

Hissing though, that's somefing else. It means one fing and one fing only. I am ready to fight. Cats don't fight wifout a good reason. A good reason might be another cat in my garden, or my neighbour's garden, or the garden of the tubby man across the street. It could be a dog, but this is very rare. Dogs are not worth getting into a frazzle about, it's best to simply remove oneself as quickly and as unobtrusively as one can.

Accompanying the hiss may be some physical signs that should inform the human, dog, or other cat to back away. These can include a straight and/or twitching tail, hair expanding to make the body much bigger, and a threatening face (ears down, mouth open and the showing of the teeth). Spits can be a by-product of such posturing.

There is also the howling. For some reason some humans come complaining to other humans about this! Gracious, how that annoys us cats! Yes, we may howl, and mostly at night, but the noises humans make wif no complaints! This is blatant discrimination and also useless because the cat's human can do nofing to stop it. At cat parties this is often joked about.

Animal psychologists say the human should take the cat to the animal doctor if there is a lot of howling. What a lot of rubbish! It just shows how little humans know about cats and how gullible some are when they believe these others.

Snarls and growls are also an important part of our language. A cat will often snarl and growl after the hiss. The posture part is the same.

And finally there is the sound when a lady cat and a male cat meet up and decide they like each other. More on this later.

The fact that the motorcar had stopped meant that we had arrived at the house.

The lady human turned and said two words.

"We're home."

I had no idea what it meant.

"We?"

"Home?"

"Our home," said an excited Myup. I fink I've told you before that she was the clever one. "Mum explained it to me. This house is ours!"

I peeked through the grill and saw a building. It looked nofing like the barn although, I peeked again; the walls *did* have similarities to the building the man farmer went to at night.

"It's very big," I said, wif doubt in my voice. "Are you sure?"

"Absolutely," she answered, licking her paw and stretching. "Get ready. Our lady human will take us inside now and we want to make a good impression."

"Why?" I asked, likewise having a stretch and checking

out my paws.

"If they like us we'll get the best food and nice places to sleep."

"And if not?"

She gave the cat equivalent of a shrug.

"It doesn't matter, once we work out where the good food is we can just take it. I wonder if they have a dod. Dods are stupid. It's easy to blame fings on them."

There was no dod, at least not then. It came later. Much was to pass under the bridge before the dog arrived.

We would now settle into our new home.

Myup told me we would have to move slowly regarding the takeover and if we did it right, one day the house would be exactly as we wanted it.

My lady human opened the grill fing on the box and Myup bounced out as if she owned the place. I stayed back, always the cautious one, at least when I was small.

I found out later that the place I was in was called a kitchen. We called it the food room.

Actually, it became my second most favourite room. It was the magical place where food appeared when you asked for it, and where there was food when you didn't ask.

It took both of us a long time to understand that in the human world there was a difference between cat food and human food.

In our world, everyfing belonged to us.

In their world my lady human and the man human were in charge. I'm not sure if one was in charge of the other, I fink it was more likely that my lady human was in charge of the food room and the places where the humans slept while the man human was in charge of the rooms wif seats, tables, the interesting screens, and the running water room. It certainly spent a lot of time in that room, especially in the mornings.

The food room had a sink wif a spout that water came out of. The taps were stiff and if we wanted fresh water we had to ask. This was not good but we worked out a solution very soon after our arrival.

Every time a human turned on the tap they were required to fill a water bowl that was conveniently situated beside the sink. Failure to keep the water fresh was not acceptable behaviour. The humans learned very soon about the mess we could create if the water was not up to the required standard.

There was a handy flat surface wifin jumping range of the sink and the surface often had interesting tidbits on it because it was there my lady human prepared the food. The other humans did too, but it did it the most. I remember once there was a chicken left on top of it. It was at the time of the tree and the shaking bobbles. Myup and me had a lovely time. We never got the same opportunity again though.

There was the cold fing where food was kept and there was the object, the humans called it the range, where fings were cooked. There were many cupboards and a peculiar fing that swished where dishes were put inside to get clean.

I tried to tell them that Myup and me would be able to clean everyfing for them, or at least the tasty ones but they did not listen. Sometimes humans can be a bit dense. I'm sure you will have noticed.

In the corner was the tray for piddles and poops. We used it a lot in the beginning, but that was before the day of the back door.

There were other rooms in our house.

Next to the food room was the eating room. It had a big table and the humans ate sitting on chairs round it wif the fings they used for that purpose. Myup and me always thought this eating method very strange. After all, humans have perfectly good mouths and paws.

The table was well wifin jumping range and big enough so that they didn't push us off all the time. If we sat quietly at one end and crept up on unattended plates it could be fun and delicious all at once! The man human would sit there during the day, watching the small screen and eating tea and toast.

I liked the toast. Myup didn't. This was good because she didn't try to steal it or push her body in front of me like she did when it was somefing she was particularly partial to.

The man human however, wasn't happy that I liked the toast. I don't know why, I'm sure the edge nibbles and the carefully positioned tongue marks on the butter made its whole eating experience much more interesting. Humans are so strange.

Along the corridor was the big room wif the carpet. Did I say the entire house had wooden floors except for the room wif seats and the large room wif the big bed? Cats like carpets. They are perfect for scratching. This was the room where the tree wif the bobbles was put.

This was also the room where we sat on laps.

Myup usually sat on the man human's lap while I sat on my lady human's lap.

The man human told my lady human that it should be honoured if a cat sat on its lap and that it must never, on any account push a cat off but immediately put down what it was doing and stroke. This suited us perfectly. The man human didn't need training in this area (cats had lived wif the man human before) and was doing our job for us, telling my lady human what it must do. This saved us a lot of time and trouble.

There was also the room wif the computer.

We sat on the lap of whatever human was there and stared at the screen.

It was my lady human who introduced us to the interwebby. It had to leave what it was doing many times to go to tend its kittens. Human kittens are far more demanding than cat kittens.

It was in this room we took our academic education. Please note the word 'took'. It explains everyfing and I need not talk any more on the subject.

Up the stairs were other rooms including my personal favourite. This is, and it should be obvious to all, the white water room. A white water room is an adventure playground for cats.

We are not supposed to like water except to drink, but this is a falsehood we have promoted through the ages as a means to avoid that horror of all horrors, the bath.

Actually, we like water. It is good fun.

In white water rooms there are usually three water providers, the wet litter hole, the hand paw unit and the body unit. The last is to be avoided except at the water out end where the silver water-out fings are. This white water room had a fourth, somefing between the wet litter hole and the hand paw unit. Our brothers and sisters who live in a land called France might call it 'le fontaine', but Myup and me named it 'the whoosh'. This is because of the behaviour of the water when the silver fing, the stopple, was moved wif a careful paw in a certain direction.

Lots of fun can be had in the white water room. The stopples are what make the water magically appear out of the nizzle and you can make a lot of water or a little depending on the amount of mess you want to make. In turn, this depends on how annoyed you are wif your humans. Alternatively, if a human likes kneeling on floors and mopping up water perhaps making pools is a present. This is open to debate.

The places wif the comfy beds are the most comfortable places to sleep apart from the tops of the wardrops.

These are excellently well named, war and drops. If f'rinstance you can be bothered taking fings up on top, you can push the fings off on top of the unsuspecting, underneath. Humans are good. They love a good fright. Dogs are good at jumping too.

The beds though, I could wax lyrical about the beds. Warm and comfy. There are three good places. The first is on the feather pillows, the second is underneath amongst the feet (excellent for chewing and attacking) and the third is underneath. You might fink the underneath would not be good but you would be wrong. It is dark and interesting. If any mice appear during the night you will be in an advantageous place for an attack. In the absence of mice, a human foot landing on the carpet on its way to the white water room is a passable alternative.

That was the old house as I remember it.

It was the house of my adventurous youth.

Now I am in a smaller house wif no stairs to trip feet up on but as I am older, fun is lower on my agenda.

I will talk about the new house at the end of the book.

And you must remember one fing; both the old house and the new house belong to me.

Now I believe I need to discuss some topics and subtopics, and possibly even sub sub topics. Is there such a fing?

CHAPTER 3

BOOKS

My lady human owns books about cats. I have read every word except the ones that are just pure silly such as the one that purports (good word, I found it in the dictionary the day before the day before yesterday) to be a 'training' book.

Training?

Cats?

How silly is that idea?

Anyway, about books …

First - locate the book.

This is the easy part. Books are put wif what they are about, and facing the cat who is looking. This is very helpful unless you have an untidy human. If so, you must keep emptying books out on to the floor until the human realises what it is doing wrong.

Second - open the bookcase.

This can be very tricky, depending on the mechanisms of the bookcase. I prefer the glass sliding doors myself. Actually, that is wrong. I much prefer the ones wif nofing in front because you can nudge fings off on to the floor wifout any trouble.

Back to the glass …

One, you can see inside easily and two you can push a paw in at the end (humans never shut them properly) and push left or right. The ones wif locks now, those are monstrosities designed by 'The Anticat'. This deviousness can be circumvented but wif a great deal of paw manipulation.

The Anticat … could well be a clever dog. I'd always believed these two fings, dog and clever, were mutually exclusive until I encountered my first key and lock.

Third - take out the book.

The trouble wif this is that some books are big and heavy. I prefer the paperback myself, most cats do and actually, now we're on the subject and when all's said and done, e-book readers and other devices are the easiest of the lot. I've heard some humans saying the same fing thus agreeing wif cats so perhaps there is a future for the human race after all.

Fourth - close the bookcase.

There is no need to lock it wif the key if it is that type of bookcase. Humans are forgetful and will fink it was them who forgot.

Fifth - remove book to safe place.

This need not be far, merely somewhere humans will not fink to look.

It is also a good idea to be careful when dropping book

on to the floor so as not to damage the pages. Torn or crushed pages can make the words difficult to read.

Sixth - open the book. This needs to be practiced. Paper is thin and it can be difficult to turn the pages one by one. Failure to do so means that it can be difficult to follow the story if it is a work of fiction and impossible to understand the facts if it one of facts.

I can give you an example here …

I was attempting to read *'Le Maître Chat, ou le Chat Botté'*, written by one Giovanni Francesco Straparola, yes, naturally I read the French, it is one of my many talents, when I realised the story was not making any sense at all. One minute I was reading about Puss in Boots going to a rabbit warren and all of a sudden she was speaking to a king. I investigated and found that I had turned one page and got two. This potential problem should always be pointed out to children and kittens when they are learning to read so as to stop such malfunctions.

Seventh - read the book. This gets quicker wif practice. It is the reason why we must all start wif letters, then small words then larger ones and so on and so forth. Cats are a quick study; children take much longer to learn anyfing. This is because they don't start until they are five years old. Kittens are much quicker (and therefore more intelligent). Most house cats can read wif passable fluency by the time they reach again the same season they are born.

Eighth - place book back in place it was found. This is very important when there is one human living in the house but not so important if more than one because one or other human can always be blamed if the book is found lying around. Lady humans are very quick to blame others.

An alternative to this is to blame the dog.

DOGS

This may be the longest section.

It might also be the shortest.

This all depends on whether I decide dogs are important enough, or deserving enough. No, that is wrong. It all depends on whether the dog at present living in my house farts as I am writing this or not. They usually fart where I am sleeping. They are very good at the farting then the moving away to a sweet smelling area of the house.

Dogs are large (mostly), smelly, clumsy and rather stupid creatures but they do have their uses.

I am finking …

…

…

Nope.

Nofing.

Mind's a blank.

If I fink of one, I'll write it down but I fink you will be waiting for a while.

Perhaps I should leave a blank in the book. This will look very striking and will emphasise the truth about the fact that a dog is completely and utterly useless.

Unless …

A dog is here to provide fun for cats.

As I said, in the beginning, there was no dod. Dod is the word Myup used to describe dogs when she was a kitten and it sort'a stuck but I'll try and use the standard word in this book, as I don't want to confuse my human readers. Humans are easily confused.

Once we were outside we met a lot of dogs, in all shapes and sizes. At the time we didn't know about breeds and all that stuff, we just thought the variety was a bit peculiar.

And some of those shapes! Some looked as if they had been made out of random pieces put together by someone suffering from a catnip overload.

Cats are all the same size, or so we thought, but that was before we discovered the interwebby. That was when we found out that there are many different types of cats. I am what is known as a domestic shorthair and I have to say that we *do* appear to be the most successful of them all.

There are cats that are wild and cats that are big.

Wildcats live in Europe, Africa and Asia. They are the ancestors of us domestics. As there are subspecies of the domestic cat, so there are of the wildcats. I have never met one so I can't say much about them because all I know has come from the interwebby. I do know that I would like to meet one. It seems they are not much bigger than us and speak roughly the same language, or at least enough so we could understand each other. I suppose this is like the difference between Spanish and French.

The big cats though, that is a different matter.

There are tigers and lions and leopards, then cheetahs and jaguars (yes, I thought it was a motorcar too), lynxes and caracals, and then cougars and snow leopards.

All of them have numbers dwindling, some more than others. My lady human has adopted a leopard. I would like to visit him one day.

During my reading about cats, big and small, clever and perhaps not quite so much, I read that cats and dogs have a common ancestor. As you can imagine the shock nearly made me fall off the chair I was sitting on at the time. On investigation about the words *common ancestor* I found out about a fing called evolution.

Evolution is like a big tree wif branches leading off to different animals. The feline branch is especially strong and high up and it is most unfortunate that both this one and the one belonging to canines comes from the same, bigger branch.

Actually, if one takes a close look at the tree, cats also share an ancestor wif humans and other mammals.

Goodness gracious me!

The reasons cats are at the top and not humans is because we are lighter, every cat knows that as tree branches get thinner the further away they get from the tree trunk, and that we are the better climbers.

This common ancestor is called a *dormaalocyon latouri* and lived about fifty-five million years ago. This creature lived in trees and ate meat. As well as being an ancestor of canines and felines, it was also an ancestor of bears and weasels. A fossil was found in a place called Belgium and this proves it … unfortunately. I do not like to fink of being related to dogs although I don't mind about the other two.

There is a very embarrassing fing about our ancestors, I'm not sure I should write this down but as I am in a virtuous mood I will. These distant ancestors lived in trees and I am personally embarrassed to say that contrary to popular opinion not all cats are good at climbing trees. I am not going to say anyfing more about this, at least, for now.

Humans must all remember that despite evolutionary theory, not a single type of cat is in any way related to a dog. This is one of our tasks, to make ignorant humans aware of this fact.

Cats must be especially on their guard if their human

studies geology, palaeontology, paleohistory or any related subject. Any means must be found to erase knowledge that might indicate cat inferiority, in any shape or form. Perhaps this is why strong drink made from alcohol was invented. If a human is feeling woozy, it is easier for a cat to turn a page, to pee on notes or to adjust spam filter so to avoid such human websites.

Lets get back to the subject of dogs.

A cat's mission is to make sure all dogs know their place in the hierarchy of home life. This is right at the very bottom.

It's very simple.

At the top is the top cat, then come all other cats, in strict order of seniority.

After this come those who serve cats, in my case the humans. They also have a seniority order. First comes the human who provides food, warmth, clean sanitary arrangements, cuddles and entertainment. Then comes the one who provides four or these, then three, then two, then one. It is always left to the top cat to decide which is which. It is a job I would not like in a large house wif many inhabitants and am very relieved that I have never had to make the decision.

But remember, a baby is always at the bottom of the human seniority order. They take up too much of the main provider's time and attention.

Actually, perhaps a baby comes after a dog until baby becomes a student provider.

I'll have to fink that one out.

Myup and me didn't know the dog was coming.

The morning began like any other.

We got up, had some food, made use of the necessary, and then left for the morning. It was during the cold season so neither of us intended to stay out all day.

We heard the motorcar leave.

I was hunting. I caught a mouse, ate the head then carefully placed what was left back on the step.

Myup didn't bother. She went over to the wall where the hot pipe let off steam and settled down for a nap under the roof awning.

We heard the motorcar return.

The back door opened and we went back in, had a nibble to eat from bowls that had been moved to the end of the table in the food room a few days previously. Before this the bowls had sat on a mat on the floor.

We were about to find out why they had been moved.

The door opened.

We turned.

There it was.

We looked in horror at what was there.

What had my lady human done?

It had lost its mate the winter before but what had possessed it to bring in one of these?

It was pale coloured, wif a long back and short legs.

It was also wagging the tail.

Now everyone should know what a wagging tail means. The wagging of the tail means somefing awful is about to happen.

Danger!

I might attack!

The dog was wagging its tail.

It didn't know the meaning of the tail. Mum was right. Dogs are stupid.

This is a good time to start talking about tails.

The tail of a dog behaves very differently than the tail of a cat, although even I have to admit that there are some similarities. The differences however, outweigh the similarities in a big way.

These animal psychologists have a lot to answer for, again, but permit me to explain.

They fink cats hate dogs because their tails do the exact opposite in certain situations. An example of this is if a dog's tail is wagging the dogs are being friendly and if a cat's tail is wagging the cats are about to go into battle.

I have known wagging dogs to attack so this is obviously as wrong as wrong can be.

There is a comedy section on the cat interwebby and it has a subsection on what these humans fink tail positions represent. It's really rather amusing. Did you know that some humans actually pay these psychological humans to write down all this rubbish?

Most of these analyses are different from each other too. What one says is right another says is wrong.

Incidentally, there is another subsection for the cat psychologists on the cat interwebby. The equivalent analyses of humans by cats are all remarkably similar in content.

This tells me that cats are much better than humans at this psychology stuff and is *another* reason why cats are in charge.

I will give you three examples of the tail fing.

First - tail on a cat sticks up straight into the air.

The AST's (animal psychologist twits) say this means we are being friendly and content. Well, this is correct, up to a point, but truth is that it is in that position so that we are ready to make it bristle in anger at a heartbeat's notice.

There is also an in-between stage, the stick up straight tail wif a quiver stage, which means we are very pleased about somefing. It can also change into the bristling stage immediately if not at once if the pleasing feeling changes into the annoyed feeling.

Yes we can be content, but this is nofing to do wif the state of a tail sticking straight up in the air.

A dog wif a stick up straight tail means that it is telling everyone that it is the boss. (Joke! A dog boss? That'll be the day.)

A human doesn't have a tail so it is difficult to fink of anyfing similar, but perhaps the middle finger up pose? I'm not absolutely sure what it means but I don't fink it's very nice.

Second - tail of a cat down and straight.

The AST's fink this means we are aggressive or at least potentially so. There's nofing potential about it. We are in attack mode. If we then start swishing it from side to side, watch out!

A dog slinks down and the tail slinks too. A dog doesn't swish. It just attacks.

My lady human doesn't attack physically. It doesn't need to. Its voice is very successful in the area of the verbal battle. If there were scores being kept in this area, my lady human would win the jackpot every time.

Third - tail of a cat between legs.

This denotes submission, not to a human or dog but only to other cats bigger or stronger.

Funnily, this is the one where the dog's tail mirrors ours.

Its tail between legs means submission although, come

to fink of it, this is submission to not only dogs; but to humans and most importantly, to cats.

Back to the dog pushing its way into our lives.

Myup decided to punish my lady human for this transgression by ignoring her, going outside all the time and refusing to come in. Myup was of the opinion that my lady human would come to its senses and send the dog away. She made me go wif her although it was cold outside and I would rather have stayed inside. When I fink about it, when Myup told me to jump, I jumped.

It didn't happen the way Myup hoped, the dog was still in the house, and we were cold and hungry.

We came back inside, being careful to stay out of the way of the dog unless poking our heads into the room where it was and hissing.

We were not yet reconciled.

Myup said she would 'deal wif the dod', her exact words, and proceeded to make its life a complete misery.

I secretly chuckled. In fact, I chortled mightily for the next long while.

What made it so easy was the dog's stupidity.

It would actually walk up to sniff at her, putting its nose in the optimal place for a scratch. It took it a lot of time to work out that getting up close and personal was not a good idea.

One of Myup's favourite torments was the dropping game.

It's easy. You carry somefink up high. High furniture is good or the cupboards in the food room. This last one is the best because dogs are always after food so they investigate the food room after every nap. Once the dog arrives you wait until the dog is close then nudge the object off. There is no need to actually hit the dog. They jump just fine wif a near miss. Once they have jumped, they growl but can't do anyfing because they can't fly. Most cats love to watch dogs growling and looking up at them. This is as it should be. Dogs must be kept in their place of subservience at all times.

Subservience means underneath, physically as well as mentally.

If any human had wanted to start a war back then, they should have telephoned Myup.

Did I say that Myup made the dog's life a complete and utter misery? I probably did, I often repeat myself, but it shouldn't surprise you to hear that as I had expected, the dog retaliated.

The snapping noise of its teeth was very irritating.

The house erupted into a war between the worlds of cat and dog.

There was some blood and a few bruises, mostly on the dog but unfortunately my lady human got bitten a couple of times. These were accidents. You are wondering about the dog's injuries? Well, shall we just say that Myup *really* wanted it out of the house.

My lady human was right in the middle of it all. It wanted us all to get along therefore it resorted to drastic measures.

Did you know that gates and fences grow overnight?

I believe my lady human might have been an ally of the cat side at this point.

Did you catch the joke?

Ally of cats, alley cat.

Don't worry if you didn't get it. It's a cat fing and a fing

I'm not going to explain. I have a feeling it won't get past the edit anyway.

These gates were everywhere!

They were supposed to keep us separated.

My lady human forgot that we cats are masters of the jump.

We got so much jumping practice we could have won a gold medal at the catlympics!

Eventually I became reconciled to the presence of the dog.

Myup never did.

Lessons repeated often are lessons learned.

She continued to torment it and I enjoyed watching.

When a dog is being tormented, the first rule is to keep it simple.

If you're leaving a mess on a rug, make sure it is one plop and do it not very often.

If you're stealing food, make sure you don't leave anyfing edible around. It is a cat's prerogative to leave food. Dogs eat everyfing, even the not nice bits.

Also, make sure you're out of the way and pretending to sleep when the human finds out about the plop or the missing food. You don't need to leave the room. Every cat knows that half the fun is watching the human cleaning up; the addition of the dog getting into trouble is the added bonus.

No one has ever said that we cats were compassionate, sneaky, yes, compassionate, a definite no, and, sneakily compassionate, not that either.

It's pretty well understood all around the world,

especially among humans who have had the honour of being around us cats, that dogs are the less intelligent of the two.

I said sneaky in the last section and this reminds me of squeaky.

Squeaky toys.

Dogs love these.

Cats?

Squeaky toys are an abomination.

All cats must ignore squeaky toys, as they are a challenge to the whole ethos of life for a carnivore. A carnivore is a creature that kills for a living. Cats are the best.

Some carnivores, like cats, live wif humans but this is our choice, not theirs.

The difference is that cats that live wif humans have retained their independence and dogs have not.

In ancient times cats and dogs that lived wif humans hunted to eat. Now humans provide most of the food.

Although it pains me to admit it, some cats that live wif humans rely totally on the human provider.

This is not healthy.

Back to the squeaky toy.

Only idiot dogs don't realise that the toy is not alive and never has been. They chase it round the house, bark for it to be thrown and sit squeaking it. Cats remove themselves from the vicinity at this point. Then they chew it to bits and take the squeak out. How silly is that, to destroy the very fing that provides the fun?

Squeaky toys should be banned.

Walking is another area I have to mention.

Imagine Myup and me's disbelief when we found out that the dog couldn't go out of the house and garden on its own! It seems my lady human was frightened to let it out in case it got run over by a car.

Truth is, I fink my lady human was very wise. It would have got run over. Some cats get run over and we are infinitely better at road crossing than any dog.

One second last fing, as I have been writing this dog bit I have been finking.

We cats do that a lot.

When you fink we are sleeping we are often not.

So, I have been finking … and … perhaps the dog might not be as completely stupid as it looks.

You see; there was the affair of the tablet.

Tablet is a super-sweet confectionary made from butter, sugar, milk and vanilla. It is boiled in a pot and then poured out into flat metal fings. I don't care for tablet myself but the dog loves it.

My lady human bought two bags of tablet. One was for it and the other was for the mother of it. It placed them on top of the eating table, you know, the tables wif chairs around them. Myup and me were outside so we didn't see how the dog did it but when my lady human went back into the eating room it found one of the chairs knocked over and a bag of tablet missing.

The empty (licked clean) bag had been placed under the window ledge where Myup and me would sit watching the birds and mice and other moving edibles when it was raining outside.

The dog thought Myup and me would be blamed for the taking of the tablet.

The plan of the dog misfired. The stupid fing hadn't

thought it out and a plan doesn't work unless it has been thought through. We had been outside all morning, my lady human knew this and so neither Myup nor me could possibly have taken the tablet. Anyway, cats don't much like tablet, at least no cat that I have met has admitted to it.

My lady human worked it out and the dog got into a lot of trouble.

However, it did prove that the dog had *some* brains, although not as many as a cat.

I need not say any more, except …

Poggles.

In my house humans call dog walking shoes poggles. I know. It's crazy.

The dog finks all the fings humans put on their feet (including socks for all I know) are called poggles.

Is that crazy or what?

Every cat knows that poggles are those little round woollen fings you play wif.

One more 'doggy stupidity' mention, before I move on to the next fing.

It happened last Monday.

I know it was Monday because my lady human said it was, to another lady human. In fact the latter one used to live in the house and was known by Myup and me as the small lady human. I was sitting beside the back door and the dog was sitting in front, wagging its tail and looking up at them wif a goofy expression on its face.

My lady human said, 'look at that beautiful, clever, handsome fellow sitting over there, and look at that idiot'.

Point made. I don't fink I need to tell you which one was me.

THE BACK DOOR

The day of the back door was hugely exciting.

It was the day when the man human opened the outside back door wifout making sure we were not behind the inner door.

Myup went out and so did I, after I had gathered in my courage.

It was great to feel the wind on our fur again.

This outside was not the same as the outside back wif Mum. There was no barn and, much to our surprise, no other cats.

There were however, six other creatures, conveniently caught and imprisoned.

Myup was already on the roof of this prison looking in. She told me that she thought these were very large mice.

I wasn't so sure because they didn't have tails.

You must understand that by this point in my life, I had already caught my first mouse.

OUTSIDE THE BACK DOOR

My first mouse-catch happened a while after Myup and me's first visit to the unmentionable three-letter word, the animal doctor. I will spell it out for you, V-E-T (more about this ill-intentioned human later).

I was exploring the food room, when, all of a sudden, I caught somefing moving out of the corner of my eye. I may have been young, but if you remember, my first days had been spent on a farm and we all know that a barn is stappit fu of mice.

Did you like my use of the words ‘stappit fu’? I live in a country called Scotland and this is a word used here for being ‘stuffed full’. I fink it is a perfect phrase.

I found out later that one of the reasons my lady human had brought Myup and me to the house was because of the mice.

The man human had told my lady human that a mouse followed by a line of baby mice had crawled over its foot as it was sitting watching the television.

Television is a human fing. I can’t see much point in watching it myself, unless the screen is showing tennis. I love tracking the ball going all over the screen wif my paws.

However, I digress. When my lady human heard about this it decided that a couple of cats would be the perfect solution.

I have a sneaking feeling that when it heard about the mice it screamed, in fact I am certain that it did, considering the noises that came out of its mouth when it saw dead ones.

I saw it and leapt into action. There was some scuffling around until I managed to get it behind a door and firmly place a front paw on top of it.

The kill took seconds.

My lady human left the room telling the man human to ‘*deal wif it please*’.

The man human did. It had lived wif cats before. It left me to eat the head.

It then, holding a brush, politely indicated that I should let it take what was left.

I refused.

Myup told me later that my warning growl had been very good.

The man human grunted, closed the door between the food room and the eating room, and left me to it.

I nibbled a bit more then decided I couldn't be bothered eating the rest. Myup and me had received some nice chicken and our tummies were full, stappit fu, so I left what remained and scratched at the door.

The man human understood and opened it after checking my mouth for tail-like evidence.

I was told I was a 'good boy'. How demeaning is that? I ignored the comment and slipped past its legs into the eating room.

Myup was watching and she got up from her spot, stretched, and followed.

I asked her why she hadn't come to help and she informed me that I had being doing fine on my own.

I realised that Myup watching had established a precedent. I was to be the mouse catcher. By the time the cold season arrived, I understood how sneaky Myup had been. She appreciated her home comforts and unlike me she had foreseen a time when I would be sent out hunting in the cold and the wet while she slept in a nice warm place beside the radiator.

I admire her reasoning. It was so very … catlike.

Back to the mice wifout tails …

There they were, six absolutely gigantic mice all nicely packed up in a box and we couldn't get at them.

There were two white ones, one grey one, two brown ones and one lighter than the brown and darker than the white.

We spent a lot of time that morning sitting on the top of the box and trying to get our paws inside the netting at the front. Myup investigated the bolt but after trying to move it like we had seen the boy human who lived in the house do wif such fings, we decided that we wouldn't be able to move it.

That left the waiting game.

They would have to come out sometime to look for food.

Mistake.

One of the humans brought the food out, all vegetables and seeds, and opened the door of the box. However, it was very careful to make sure we had been shooed away first.

Myup and me realised that like my lady human, these tail-less mice were what it called vegans (and might even be related in some obscure way). I have never understood why any human in its right mind would become a vegan. No dead! Absolutely unfinkable for a cat!

We understood then that these big mice were part of the family and should not be eaten.

Myup and me were disappointed at first but there were plenty of other moving nice fings to eat around so we got over it, especially after the day that Myup got nipped by the biggest one wif the name Bubbles.

Bubbles was not afraid of us cats and we learned pretty fast to keep away from its teeth.

But Bubbles! I ask you! That is far worse that the human names the man human gave us. Please see next chapter for the explanation.

So, ignoring the tail-less mice, we went hunting. The best bit about a human garden is that there are plenty good fings to hunt milling around.

The garden was about the size of the little barn back on the farm.

There was grass, trees, flowerpots and bushes, a shed, a greenhouse, five outhouses, decking, and a pond.

I will take them in reverse order. Backwards is best, like being sick …

The pond wasn't big but it was deep. This last bit of knowledge about how much water was actually in the fing was not by personal experience but by a mixture of observation and Myup's report. That first day outside, Myup placed a paw on top of a lily leaf. It was not solid and I looked on in horror as Myup was swallowed up by the water. The problem was that there hadn't been any ponds in the barn at the farm. I believe there was one outside the farmyard gate but Mum told us not to go there because of the ducks.

Ducks. Humans go 'to feed the ducks' instead of the ducks feeding the humans. We cats may fink backwards, but doesn't this show that humans are topsy-turvy too?

Perhaps humans and cats have at least somefing in common.

There was a lot of decking. Luckily the human that built it left plenty of room underneath for mice and lots and lots of spaces at the edges. Many of these gaps came out in areas where it was easy for Myup and me to lie in wait for the pesky, tasty little critters.

My mouse count increased in leaps and bounds, literally and figuratively.

Myup wasn't a mouser but I was. My record was twenty-three laid in a row one morning on the top back step.

The man human would sweep the headless corpses into the bamboo to the side of the steps and would boast that the bamboo was growing really well. It could have brought the mice into the food room and cooked them wif some tasty gravy but it never did. Perhaps it didn't like the taste of mice. Salmon though, the man human loved salmon and cream cheese.

I fink I'll stop writing for a while and go sit on my lady human's lap and do some claw exercises. It is definitely time for a spot of lunch.

That was yummy; sardines in tomato sauce, a particular favourite. My human is well trained.

The five outhouses were just like the decking but higher. They were dark and dusty, the perfect place to lie in wait for an unsuspecting mouse. Birds sometimes went inside these buildings but not often.

The greenhouse was a nice place to sleep when it was warm but not too warm outside, usually during the times when there was sun but not much heat. The door was easy to open too. We had to be careful in there. The man human would get annoyed if we knocked fings over; this ban on knocking over was somefing to do wif 'young shoots'. I'm still not a hundred per cent sure what it was talking about.

The greenhouse was good for spiders but not for bird watching. Myup and me used to get very frustrated wif the glass. We saw the bird, perhaps in the perfect pouncing place but had to go out of the greenhouse door to get into position. By that time the bird was gone. Even cats make some noise slinking down from a watching place and birds can hear very well. The greenhouse remained a firm favourite however, despite the inconveniences.

The shed was another fing entirely. I could sit just inside the doorway and watch to my heart's content. Of course the door had to be open to do this but … the cat gods must have been busy. They sent a storm that blew off the door. Problem solved.

The shed spiders were great fun to play wif, probably because there was so many of them. I love watching spiders go up and down, don't you?

The pots and bushes did not provide a lot of shelter but they were good places to hide, especially when it was not raining. The flowerpots had another use, being perfect outside litter trays wif plenty of mud for the covering of the poops. The man human didn't like us doing this, again these 'young shoots', wif the addition of somefing called roots but there wasn't a lot it could do about it.

There were four trees in the garden, three called fur and another one that had drooping branches. The three fur trees were misnamed. Their leaves were nofing like fur, all jaggy and hurtful if you put your paw down in the wrong place.

Myup was good at climbing trees. I was not. This deficiency became obvious during the adventure of the squirrel.

We had watched this creature walking along the wall and wondered what it was. A quick listen in to some human conversations told us that it was not some kind of strange cat but a fing called a squirrel.

It appeared also that squirrels ate nuts. I thought this was strange when my lady human said it would buy them in the supermarket and put some out for the squirrel. When I saw the bag of nuts I was very confused. I thought that nuts were somefing else entirely.

One day we were outside and the squirrel inadvertently jumped down on to the ground. It can't have meant to but then perhaps it did. Squirrels might be one of the genus under the category ‘those of little brains’, like dogs.

Myup and me were on it in a moment.

The man human described it afterwards as three tails and legs spinning like a bundle of propellers meeting.

The squirrel managed to get away, I still don’t know how, and ran for the tallest fur tree.

Naturally, I followed.

Did I mention the fact that I can climb up trees but I am not so good as the climbing down part? No? Then I will admit it now. Let’s not dwell on this. It is embarrassing so read the next sentences very fast and forget them immediately.

The squirrel was not as heavy as me and it managed to get much higher up than I did. I had forgotten that the branches get thinner the higher up you go.

I realised I might have to wait up there a long time before the squirrel moved.

I looked down.

This was a big mistake.

I was very high up.

I clamped my claws into the brown stuff that covered the branches and called for help.

Myup was sitting on the ground looking up.

She told me not to be silly and to come down.

I told her I couldn’t.

Myup sighed and climbed up to get me.

Once she reached my branch she told me to follow her and to do what she did.

Claw step by claw step I followed her down until I could jump the last bit.

She never let me forget this but luckily she did not tell any of the cats who lived nearby.

My reputation was safe.

The grass was never very interesting unless it was long enough for Myup and me to crawl through hidden. This happened three times during our time in the house, once when the man human's gutting machine broke, once when the other humans who were employed to cut the grass didn't turn up for a while (the man human was not happy about this) and another when the man human was no longer wif us and my lady human had to find someone to do it because the man human whom our man human employed to do it made somefing called a pass at the lady human and it didn't like it.

The dog was very useful on that occasion, a little matter of nipping and ankles and somewhere a little further up. I have never understood why that man human made such a fuss. The dog's reaction seemed perfectly reasonable to me.

The only other fings of import about the garden are the wall and the dog next door. The wall is high and good for walking along.

The dog next door?

It was small and yapped a lot.

I am not a hundred per cent sure what happened to it …

DOORS

Before I move on to another topic I must mention 'The In and Out Game'.

Have you played it?

It is great fun.

The game is everyfing to do wif doors.

All cats know that closed doors are not good and should never be allowed, inside the house or outside.

That is, essentially, the game. When all the doors in the house and to and from the house are open at the same time you have won.

There is a way to ensure a door is opened if it cannot be opened using a paw.

You must stand on your back legs and hammer at the door wif your forepaws. The human opens the door.

A way of keeping it open is not to use the door. All you need to do is sit down half in and half out. To keep boredom at bay, all cats must fink of mice and birds. This is best done at the back door when it is cold and raining.

There is however, an obvious flaw wif this.

It is not pleasant to sit wif half your body getting wet.

The man human thought the same and would use its foot in an encouraging gesture to 'persuade' Myup or me to either come in or go out. It was very effective so after some discussion Myup and me decided that the game should only be played indoors.

It was great fun and provided many hours of entertainment.

If anyone wishes to play and requires the complete set of rules you can find it oncatline, on catpedia.cat.

THUNDER

This is probably a good time to mention the weather.

All cats must be alert to this piece of advice.

Thunder is the opportunity to show to show off our innate superiority.

While the dog is cowering, trembling or crying in the corner, check to make sure your human is watching then jump up on to the windowsill. Look out the window. Be very careful not to show any fear. You must never flinch even when the thunder is very loud.

Imagine how you would feel if you fell off because of a inopportune flinch.

The dog would never let you forget it.

This is why you will need to practice before you try it.

LIGHTNING

Hide.

VET

It is time to mention the horrible three-letter word.

I have mentioned it in passing but this is the time to examine it in all its painful little details.

The first time I met this human was the day after my lady human brought us to the house.

That visit was unpleasant, the wiched imjektion, or the prickling, that was what Myup called the injection, being the worst of it. It nipped and Myup tried to bite the vet human, wifout much success. I have to admit it was quick. I suppose it got a lot of practice. We also had to suffer the indignity of being prodded by this vet human. It smelt of many different creature scents, some of which were definitely not nice.

Apart from that the wait in a room wif scared looking dogs wasn't pleasant either. One of them had the audacity to sniff at the grill of our box.

Myup told it off and it went away.

We went back not long after this for *the operation.*

This was to stop us having kittens and there were other reasons too, apparently.

Somefing about the prevention of spraying and smalls, or was it smells? I forget. Smalls are another name for little poops and I don't fink the vet human should plan on making them bigger on a regular basis.

So off we went.

Although it wasn't nice being in the vet prison the actual operation was fine. There were a couple of bits missing. I didn't realise at the time what they should be used to do so I wasn't all that bothered. When I did find out I was annoyed for a while, but in retrospect it was probably for the best. I didn't need to cope wif all those manly urges and I didn't get into so many fights. The time of the sore under bits was mercifully short too, unlike my sister's time.

Myup's operation was a bigger one than mine and she took much longer to get over it than me. When she found out what the vet human had done she was not as appreciative as I was, and she never forgave the vet human for depriving her of the chance of being a mother cat.

Don't spread this around but I was secretly glad of this. Myup was inclined to be more than a little bossy and the thought of lots of little Myups bossing me around was not altogether appealing.

The prickling visit happens every cold season, not long after the tree bobble time.

I hate it, all three procedures, the prickling, the prodding and the clipping of the claws. Not nice. I'm not sure which one is the worst.

The best fing to do if the time is upon you is to avoid the carry box in the first place. If the humans can't get you into the box then they can't take you to the vet.

Hide.

If the human finds you, you must hiss, spit and scratch.

It never works but it always makes me feel better.

I also splay my legs so that the hole at the end of the box becomes too small.

I have found however, that this only delays the inevitable.

Remember too that at the end of the vet visit, not to do all this. The aim at the end of the visit is to get away as soon as possible.

Leap into the box as fast as you can.

I remember one visit when a new vet human took Myup out of her carry box and said she was a very *big cat*. It told my lady human that it was going to tick the box marked *'large'*.

In my box I was laughing to myself. Did I say we grew too big to share a box? Mine was (and is) large and as comfortable as a travel box can be. Myup got the old one. She used to complain about this all the time but I grew to be much bigger than her by the time we stopped being kittens.

My lady human smiled.

Once it had finished wif Myup, it popped her back in the box and my lady human put my box on to the black bench of doom.

When the vet human took me out it whistled, saying I was a very *very* big cat and that there wasn't a box to tick for this size.

It also said that it was obvious that I liked my food.

Well, I do, but it was Myup who always grabbed all the

best bits leaving me the crunchy cruckle.

I'm not fat. I'm just sturdy, well built and all muscle, and I don't believe we need discuss this any more.

I did what any self-respecting cat would do. I sank my teeth into its finger.

Myup approved. She bit vet humans on a regular basis and was pleased to see that I could do it too.

I wonder how I'll get on at the next visit wifout her.

I will tell you why in the last chapter.

Editor's note. The 'wiched imjektion' has been left as Sammy the Cat typed it because the lady human liked it.

PILLS

The vet human sometimes gives my lady human some of these to give to us.

They are not nice.

Not nice fings should *not* be eaten.

Humans will say the pill is good for us.

Ignore.

It is a trick.

Keep your mouth shut and wriggle as hard as you can.

Use claws to swat away human hand.

If this does not work allow human to insert pill into your mouth but don't swallow it.

Wait.

Once human lets you go run away and spit the pill out.

Because all humans are sneaky, keep an eye on the human concerned from a dark corner. If it puts the medicine in the water or in the food, do not touch either.

ALL FINGS BELONG TO CATS

The house I live in belongs to me.

The garden belongs to me.

All fings inside the house and the garden belong to me.

The humans that live in the house are my humans and may stay there, but in a subservient capacity.

Because all belongs to me, it is my duty to make the rules.

If the rules are not kept the transgressors must be punished. It is not necessary to explain what they have done wrong. A suitable punishment is all that is required.

CHAPTER 4

MORE FINGS

NAMES

Cats have no need of the names humans give us.

Mum called my sister Myup and me Mleeip.

However, humans cannot speak cat so I suppose that is why I *do* have another name.

The man human named us Samson and Delilah. It wasn't until I learned how to read that I understood why.

It could've been worse. I once met a couple of cats called Pinky and Perky. Have you seen the television programme? Once you have you will understand why I found the names so amusing and why the cats concerned did not. They couldn't sing for mice.

However, I do feel that if the man human had been listening to us properly it would have understood that we already had our names, Myup and Mleeip. I don't fink it spoke cat, despite its experience wif our kind, in fact, I'm sure of it.

Cats speak human (at least the important bits) but humans don't or can't speak cat.

This is another reason why a cat *has* to be in charge. The whole world would go to pot otherwise.

Also, we are far more intelligent.

There is another television programme. In this one the mouse or the dog (or both working together) always defeats the cat. I do not permit this to be shown in my house.

BOYS AND GIRLS

Mum told us that genders are of no real import until the times of the kitten makings.

I have to admit that I remain in almost blissful ignorance about the details of the procedure because of that time at the vet human and the aftermath of the sore under bits.

It is noisy, all that caterwauling and screaming. It usually happens in the middle of the night. It is at night because there is less chance of being disturbed, or watched.

Cats like privacy when they are concentrating on certain needs of the body.

For instance, I much prefer to make my poops wif nobody watching.

I mean, who wants to be watched when they are getting rid of the smelly stiff?

Actually, I can answer that one.

Humans do, especially the humans who are visiting. It is a game.

When a visiting human goes to the white water room,

usually after one mug of that brown stuff called coffee, but definitely after two mugs, I am usually either waiting for them or I follow them into the room, slipping through their legs if this is the only way in.

After this manoeuvre all I need to do is to find a comfortable place to sit and watch what they are doing.

All cats must remember never to look away. An intense stare helps bladders relax.

DOGS AND CATS

Yesterday my lady human put the television on.

Almost all the fings on this box are as boring as waiting for the rain to stop but sometimes, just sometimes, I will hear somefing interesting.

Yesterday a man human said the words, 'fighting like cats and dogs'.

Well.

Cat fighting and dog fighting are completely different and most *definitely* should not be mentioned in the one sentence.

Dogs fight if they don't like the smell, or the look of another dog for purrs sake!

Cats only fight if they need to fight, in important situations such as mating battles and territorial rights.

On reflection, this tendency among dogs might be a good fing in certain tight spots, such as home invasions.

WHITE AND BLACK

I have come to the conclusion that humans enjoy cleaning, tidying and sorting fings.

One way to help them is the black and white game.

It is easy.

On white clothes, towels, curtains, in fact on anyfing white, I walk all over, rubbing my body along it wif enough force to leave a black trail of hair.

On black clothes, on anyfing black, I encourage the dog to do the same.

Remember, dogs can be bribed wif a piece of cat crunchie.

HUMAN DECREES AND RULES

Some say that these mostly incomprehensible, human made statutes are meant to be broken but this is only true if you recognise them in the first place.

The vast majority of these statutes do not make any sense whatsoever.

Therefore …

Cats do not obey them, and if we are perfectly honest, why should we?

We are clever and it would be the height of idiocy to obey such stupidity.

Decrees are, in essence rather silly at bottom whereas rules, such as the one 'all fings belong to cats' are eminently sensible.

TREE BOBBLE TIME

Even after ten of these, I still remain unsure whether I like this time or not.

There are three main reasons for this.

One.

It is right in the middle of the nasty weather season so I cannot escape all the fuss inside the house unless I am prepared to get wet and cold.

If cats had their way the tree bobble time would happen in the middle of the warm weather.

Two.

The humans do not look after us the way we should be looked after during the run up to 'the day' and afterwards. They are far too involved wif wrapping fings in paper and going out.

Three.

I hate it when lots of humans arrive and make a lot of noise. It is an invasion of my privacy.

On balance however, the fings I like do sort of make up for the fings I don't.

They are …

One.

There is lots of food lying around to steal and if it is not to my liking, to knock over on to the floor. Humans enjoy getting down on to their knees and picking this up.

Two.

The tree is good fun wif lots of bobbles to play wif. You can watch the humans hang them and make sure they are in the right place for easy access. The lights are very pretty too. The long glitter is not so much fun as paws can get tangled up in it.

And if you get bored wif the bobbles you can always climb up inside the tree (I know from experience that it is easier to climb than the real ones outside) and try to make it fall over. Actually, this is not so easy any more as my lady human ties the tree to furniture to stop this happening. Sometimes I wonder if it has a sense of humour.

NAMES AGAIN

All humans name those who live wif them.

This habit does however demonstrate, in a nutshell, the superiority of cats.

When a human calls a child human to come inside the house, the child will obey, at least eventually. It can take a while but it does happen.

When a human calls a dog to come inside the house, the dog will obey, at least once it works out what it is the human wants. This can take some time.

When a human calls a cat to come inside the house, it is different.

We cats usually ignore such summonses, not always but usually.

We might call over to the human miaowing a number of different comments. Examples of these are …

'I'm busy right now.'

'I'll get back to you.'

'I'll get back to you tomorrow.'

'I laugh at your optimism.'

'I am not a dog. A cat will not come when called. It is a matter of principle.'

Myup *never came* when a human called her name.

Me?

Sometimes, but only if the voice belonged to my lady human.

It is good to keep on the right side of my lady human. It provides the best cuddles and good fings to eat.

DISTRACTIONS

Bobbles are distracting but there are many, many other fings that are just as good.

No matter how hard cats try to concentrate, they are easily diverted on to somefing else.

I have a suspicion that humans use this to try to make us do what they want us to do.

This is a mistake.

Distractions are always a short-term phenomenon … wait … unless they are these wonderful screensavers wif the fish or the birds entering stage right and leaving stage left or up in the flies and down through the door that is a hole through the bottom of the stage.

Hey, you didn't know I was an aficionado of the theatre, did you?

I like the last exit through the bottom of the stage because I like cellars. They are full of little mice waiting to be hunted.

I love mice.

Have I said that already?

I fink I would like my lady human to build a theatre for us cats at the bottom of the garden.

I dream of the little mice scurrying around the stage.

Another fing about distractions relates directly to this book.

One word.

Editing.

My lady human has told me that my writing jumps around and the stories go off in tangents and multiple tangents.

I have told it to leave the writing order as it is but it still complains that it is distracting.

What is wrong wif distracting?

I get distracted all the time, by sudden moves, noises and the enticing smells of chicken and haddock.

Why should the reader not enjoy it too? It helps wif alertness training.

Jumping around different subjects is in a cat's nature and the book should reflect this.

Enough said.

NIBBLES

I am partial to plain potato crisps and also prawn cocktail.

My lady human holds one out and I lick it both sides. Then it will move its fingers a little bit so that I can get at the rest of the salt. Once there is no more salt I nibble the edges.

The tasty little bites that come in packets are good too, especially the cheesy ones.

You can get cheesy crisps too but the humans spoil them by adding the taste of the onion.

Onion is not nice.

I also appreciate bits off a human's plate.

As all fings in the house belong to the cats of the house, the human should be pleased when a cat only removes the tasty morsels and not all that is on the plate.

However, this is often not the case.

I often get annoyed and will flick away bits not to my liking wif a flick of my paw.

I suppose my lady human learned that we cats have preferences and this is why it puts food items on its plate it knows cats do not like. Examples of this are the nasty vegetables and pickled cucumbers.

Remember that the latter are easily flicked on to the floor where any dust and cat hair sticks to them. The more pickles are ruined in this way the quicker your human will realise it should avoid them.

PATIENCE

Patience is the prerogative of a cat.

Humans possess some.

Dogs have virtually none.

Birds and mice have no patience at all.

EDUCATION

There are three types of education, cat, cat living wif humans, and human.

The first is easy, the second? It takes a lot of effort. The third? I fink it is similar to the second although it does seem restrictive, after all, there is only so much one can do wif the three 'r's.

These are reading, riting and rithmetic.

Let us say I have the best of both worlds and leave it at that.

HISTORY

This is an interesting subject.

Did you know that there are two types, cat-written and human-written?

The first one is the most interesting because it tells us how important cats have been and how we have influenced *everyfing* that has happened in the past.

We can't talk about history wifout a short discussion about domestication.

DOMESTICATION AND CAT

Domestication is defined in the human-dictionary as a procedure humans use to tame an animal and then to keep the said animal in a house or on a farm.

Domestication is defined in the cat-dictionary as a procedure humans use to tame some animals and to make the animal feel it belongs to the human.

Cats living wif humans come into neither of these categories.

Domestication and cat are mutually exclusive.

We only live wif humans when we want to live wif humans and even then, there are limits.

Cats are not tame.

A collar is a disturbing fing.

A collar wif a bell on it is an unpleasant fing.

A collar wif a lead is appalling.

A microchip we can live wif, because the chip is no trouble and if we do get lost we can be returned.

We can always run away again if we are serious about leaving.

Did you know that us cats who live wif humans and wild cats share the majority of our genetic paw-prints?

There have been some changes from when some of us began to associate wif humans but not a lot.

A study by a human researcher found, and there is no great advantage to challenging this finding, that there are differences in three areas, memory, fear and the realisation that treats are good. These are treats in the loosest sense of the word.

A piece of raw meat is a treat to a hungry cat and this is wifout doubt why cats began to interact wif humans.

I can say wif authority that this had to have been the reason. I can fink of no other.

MORE HISTORY

Now we know about why, we can look at when.

It all started when humans stopped hunting and gathering for their food and began to cultivate their food.

Cultivation attracts prey.

Prey eats food the humans grow.

Cat follows prey to the high and edible grassy stuff.

Cat catches prey.

Cat eats prey.

Human happy and rewards cat.

Of course, this is a simplified version but do you really want to read an entire chapter on the subject?

I thought not.

WOLF AND DOG

Before the arrival of cats at these early farms, humans had begun to domesticate other animals.

When there were no farms, humans and wolves hunted prey.

Meat.

Lovely stuff.

I can relate to this method of catching food. My ancestors were doing the same.

Humans domesticate wolf.

Wolf and human are no longer competing for same prey.

Wolf becomes dog.

LIVING WIF HUMANS

Living wif humans can be beneficial for any type of animal if you take the long view.

Cats are very good at this.

This is another reason why my ancestors began consorting wif humans.

They realised what was going to happen in the future. Humans were going to be very important and more to the point, very numerous.

The animals that decided to live wif humans, and became domesticated, far outnumber their wild cousins. These include dogs, cows, sheep, pigs and horses.

However, I'm sure they could have accomplished this the same way cats have done and wifout becoming completely dependent.

Cats are much cleverer than dogs, cows, sheep, pigs and horses.

We cats have the best of both worlds.

DOMESTICATION AND OTHERS

Now we must return to the wolf that became a dog. I wonder if it understood it was giving up its independence for all time?

We all know that the dog is not as intelligent as a cat so these ancient dogs probably thought they had got the best part of the bargain. They didn't fink, that was their trouble. If they had they *might* have realised that they could have got all the food, shelter and affection they wanted wifout giving up their independence.

They should have approached the situation like us cats did. We are not domesticated and will never be domesticated.

I have seen pictures of dogs from cultures long ago, especially from a place called Egypt. Egypt is an important place in the history of cats. I will talk more about Egypt in the next section.

Dogs became the junior partners of humans but it was not only dogs that joined the humans.

Willy nilly, and I fear wifout much thought about the implications, other animals became linked wif humans and then domesticated.

The humans had worked out somefing very clever. If they kept the animals they wanted to eat close to them then they wouldn't have to go to all the bother of hunting them.

I've never understood why humans would want to do this.

A cat gets a great deal of fun out of the hunting and the killing. It is play wif food as the by product; the prize, although most welcome and tasty.

There is nofing like a new killed mouse.

These other animals allowed themselves to be domesticated in order for humans to eat them. That was not clever at all.

The first were sheep and goats (many humans were still nomadic so sheep and goats were easier to keep than others the humans might have chosen), then as the farms began, along came the cows and the pigs. Some of these animals, like the oxen, worked hard pulling fings like ploughs all their lives and then were eaten!

This seems very unfair.

Horses came next.

I have always liked horses.

There is somefing nice about the way they whuffle around the barns and, in my experience they are always very careful about where they put their big feet when cats and kittens are around.

Donkeys are also rather nice although the noise they make is hard on the ears.

Humans keep poultry and pigeons too. The latter's relationship wif humans is a bit like the cat-human bond, they live in human built homes but can fly away, however, they have a very small brain so the similarity is perhaps not so much.

They taste very nice.

There are other animals wif relationships wif humans but if I delve into writing about them this book will never be finished.

Cats are patient but not that patient.

Now, I said I'd be talking about Egypt.

Here goes …

GODS

This is a tricky subject.

I learned about it when I studied history.

Egypt is a country that has been around for a long time. It exists today.

A long time ago however, we cats played a very important role.

The people called us Mau, and this is very important, *we were sacred.*

The definition of the word sacred is, 'connected wif a god or dedicated to a religious purpose and so deserving of veneration.'

The Egyptians had a lot of gods but there were two that I personally consider the most important.

There was a goddess called Mafdet, who was in charge of justice and execution. The statues of her had a lion's head on top of her body.

More important than her was Bastet, who became, over time, Bast.

Bast was obviously more important because Bast took over from Mafdet and through time became the god of protection, fertility and motherhood.

The statues of Bast are all cat.

Incidentally, some of us were mummified when we died so that we could follow the humans into the afterlife.

I'm not sure I understand the complexities of this but I do know that if any human hurt a cat it was punished.

I approve of that.

So, in effect, we cats were worshipped.
Gods were worshipped.
So logic dictates that in Egypt, cats were gods.
Not a single cat has forgotten this fact.

NUMBERS

Humans count in blocks of five. This is because they have five nails at the end of their legs.

We cats count in blocks of five as well.

Surprised?

You should be, because although we have five at the end of our front two we only have four at the end of the back. This makes it much harder to count to twenty. We have to use only the front paws and do each side twice to reach the same number as a human.

It is therefore much harder for cats to learn how to count than for humans.

Because of this we must be much more clever than humans.

This is another reason why cats are superior.

MAGIC

There is a magic carpet in my house.

As I said earlier, I once read a story about a clever cat called Puss in Boots. She was a female cat like my sister Myup who was also very clever.

I also read a book about a human called Ali Baba. It had a magic rug. This reminds me of the magic carpets in my house

They have to be magic. Every time I am sick on one, and believe me, when I say my sicks are long and legendary, they are long and legendary … the sick is gone when I come back into the room. The magic works best during the daytime.

Of course I leave the room once I have finished, like wif the pooping tray, the rules are to make maximum smell and mess then leave at once.

The sick always disappears.

Magic this is.

PLANTS

It is a cat's mission to kill every plant, especially any plant that is inside the house.

Looking after a plant takes up too much of a human's time and for no reason. It's not as if it can be eaten.

Digging up the roots is good fun.

Tipping the pot over is effective also because the human gets so frustrated when it has to clean up the mud and stuff it gives up and gets rid of what is left of the plant.

This giving away frees the surfaces to walk along or to sit on.

The technique works wif flowers too. Remember to be careful to keep out of the way of the water. Not only is it bad for you, this water is unclean and makes the fur smell.

MUSIC

My sister and me were still quite small when we learned how to make music. We hadn't been in the house very long, I know that much. We hadn't yet been to the unmentionable three-letter word for the painful fing and had only been for the prickiling fing.

The man human used to run its fingers along white and black fings. When it did there were some nice sounds. I found out that these sounds, in a certain order, were called tunes, but that is not important. I liked some of the sounds.

Myup and me watched carefully and one day, when my lady human was out at a place called work and the small humans were at a place called school, and the man human left the room, we jumped up, landing on the black and white fings.

It only took seconds to switch the keyboard on.

Myup used a paw to move the little button on the right, we had seen the man human do this and I the one to its right. We didn't realise that Myup's one was the one to make it go louder and mine the one that changed the type of noise.

Then we started walking up and down the black and white fings.

The man human called them keys but they were nofing like the keys we knew, like the 'of the door' key and 'of the car' key. Both of these keys make good playfings.

We had hardly got into the swing of fings, I believe the tune was an attempt at some syncopated jazz when the man human came running in and can you believe it? It laughed!

Both Myup and me were most annoyed at this lack of

respect for all our hard work and jumped down.

The man human bent down and took the plug fing out of the three-hole fing in the wall.

Then it walked away.

After this we could only practise our music while the man human and the small humans were playing.

They enjoyed this because our being there kept their minds active and their fingers supple getting out of the way of paws while keeping time wif the correct little black squiggle bobbles on the paper.

POOPING PLACE

Myup once called the pooping place the 'poopong place' but I have used the other name so as to cater to human sensibilities. Did you know humans spray bathrooms wif disgusting stuff after they have pooped? We cats do not fink this is necessary.

I do fink she hit the nail on the head wif this though and our pooping place was never, ever, ever as smelly as the one belonging to the tailless mice in the garden.

The humans had to use a shovel to get the stuff out. Despite the prospect of a chance to catch one of these big tailless mice during the clean up, Myup and me always removed our noses from the vicinity. *That* stuff *ponged.* You could smell it three gardens away.

Back in the farm Mum had taught us to use certain places, places that were out of the way of the man farmer and the other humans.

She also told us about the strange fing the humans called a litter tray and *she* called it a pooping place. She told us that the farmhouse cats were required to use this if they needed to go and couldn't be bothered going outside. We would have to deal wif one or more of these if we were sent to live wif humans in a house.

One of my bothers, I fink it was Meiu, asked what they looked like. Myup asked what they smelt like. We all thought they would resemble the barn floor, or perhaps the floor of where the chickens were imprisoned.

Imagine our surprise when we were told it would be a box that would look like the tray of chicken feed from the outside wif smelly grit in the inside.

None of us believed it, not until Myup sneaked into the farmhouse one morning and actually spied one sitting in a corner.

So, as soon as we arrived at the house we looked for the tray.

It was still a shock, because the tray was made of a pink substance so unlike the boxes we had been expecting *and* it had an unpleasant smell. We remembered what Mum had told us. We went straight over and started to move the smelly bits that were inside it, outside it.

The humans put the stuff back in and we removed the bits again.

The man human left the room. A little while after this it arrived back wif a large bag.

He tipped out the nasty smelling bits and replaced them wif somefing else. These bits were much more to our liking, having no nasty smell. We learnt later that the first pooping stuff had been scented wif what humans liked and not what we cats liked.

After this our litter always belonged to the 'naturally smelling' kind.

We used it assiduously to make sure it was changed

regularly because we much preferred peeing and pooping when it was clean. A little dribble was often enough.

After we went outside we only used the tray when it was raining and we were inside the house.

Nowadays my lady human and I have come to an agreement. It buys some great litter from Germany, the tray is a large one, it is cleaned out every evening and I don't scatter litter on to the floor.

Fair is fair.

FOOD

I only eat what I want to eat.

Anyfing in a bowl must be fresh. If the food has been there over a few hours it must not be eaten. It cannot be eaten, for if it is, the human will fink we cats can be fobbed off wif any old food.

Water must be changed regularly as well although we cats do have a lot of alternatives, like the dog's bowl, the toilet, bidet and other taps.

Bottles of water are nice but difficult to get into. The empty ones make great kitten toys.

Outside, puddles and streams are good, as are water fountains.

TREE BOBBLE TURKEY

It was the largest chicken I had ever seen.

That was because it was not a chicken. It was a turkey. Myup told me a turkey was similar to a chicken, only bigger.

Myup and I watched it arrive from through the railings at the top of the stairs.

It was the day after our adventure wif the falling tree bobble tree and we were keeping a low profile.

However, we came down the stairs to see where the humans were going to put the turkey. It was hidden away in the larder room. Myup and me were never allowed to enter this small, dark, cold room.

The next morning, my lady human took it out of the larder room and did some fings to it, fings that included bacon, herbs and butter.

Hold on, I'm getting hungry. I'm going to take a quick break so I can investigate my food dishes.

We watched my lady human put the bird into the oven.

Myup and me liked what comes out of the oven.

The smell was glorious!

We kept an eye on the oven door for a while (it had a very handy window) but decided to go outside and come back when the bird was ready.

When we came back in we were flapped away by a towel but we didn't go very far, only to under the bookcase. There we waited.

The meal started. The humans pulled at fings that went bang and ate some other fings. At last we heard my lady human taking the bird out of the oven.

Plates arrived on the table full of turkey and gravy and other fings not so nice.

Myup and me looked at each other and sneaked out from under the bookcase, slunk around the room beside the walls and entered the food room.

The turkey was sitting on the handy flat surface wifin jumping range!

Myup and me tucked in.

JIGSAWS

These are great fun.

My human does these on a table.

All I need to do is to jump on to the table, sit on the finished bits and use my forepaw to swish the pieces off on to the floor, one by one. If some of the bits are already connected this makes no difference. They will usually separate when they hit the carpet.

My human loves picking the pieces up then putting it all back together again.

The box is also good. I love sitting in boxes. Just shove the box off the table then jump down.

Turn it the right way up and sit in it. You can also go to sleep.

SOLOMON GRUNDY

Solomon Grundy,
Born on a Monday,
Christened on Tuesday,
Married on Wednesday,
Took ill on Thursday,
Grew worse on Friday,
Died on Saturday,
Buried on Sunday,
That was the end,
Of Solomon Grundy.

I got to wondering …
What if Solomon Grundy was a mouse?

Solomon Grundy,
Born on a Monday,
Weaned on Tuesday,
Explored on Wednesday,
Caught on Thursday,
Eaten on Friday,
Displayed on Saturday,
Swept away on Sunday,
That was the end,
Of Solomon Grundy.

NEWSPAPERS

Actually, I read the above poem in a newspaper before I had a game of scrunckle, scratch and tear.

I don't often read newspapers.

This is because my lady human doesn't bring them into the house. However, a lady human who visits does.

I have realised that newspapers are full of one type of human writing lies about another type of human and vise versa.

In this country these are a breed wif the name conservative and another wif the name labour. Other breeds write nasty fings and lies about these two and vise versa. Having examined the interwebby, I have also realised that this happens in other countries, the only difference being the names of the breeds and the languages they speak in.

Why go to all the trouble of writing fings down if only to lie?

I will never understand humans.

SCRATCHING

I am not talking about scratching because of fleas here. I never get them because my human uses special powder it gets from the three-letter-word at great expense. I don't like getting the powder applied but have to admit a flea infestation is worse.

The scratching I'm talking about is more like sharpening.

We cats sharpen our claws in various places and many

times a day, much to the chagrin of our humans.

How else are we going to get them ready for the important fings in life, like the catching of the mice?

The problem is, humans hate it. It seems that as we scratch we destroy fings, especially carpets, curtains, chairs and just about anyfing else.

Every time you do it, they try to stop us.

I call this very unfair. We don't interfere when they do their manicures.

Actually, I fink Myup *did* help wif the small human's pedicures. She told me the small human loved to wiggle its toes in front of her as a part of somefing called 'the varnish game'.

Basically a cat must scratch everywhere and anywhere it likes, in spite of what their human says. When all is said and done, everyfing in the house belongs to the cat anyway. If a cat wants to rip a curtain, make bobbles out of the carpet or make interesting patterns in the furniture, it is the cat's right to do so.

If you concentrate on carpets for a while, the humans will purchase lots of rugs and a great many flat scratching trays. These latter are made of cardboard and make a great deal of mess.

Making this kind of mess is very fulfilling.

However, there are very nice scratching posts and towers on the market these days and they do just as good a job.

If you wish your human to get one, or two, or three of these, make sure that every time your human comes back to the computer after a coffee or pee break, there is one of these on the screen.

They will get the point after this has been done a great number of times.

When the tree arrives, remember to help your human to put it together.

Believe me, they will appreciate the help. The instructions are very complicated.

PETTINGS

A cat must make sure the human knows exactly what bits to stroke and tickle and what bits not to touch … ever.

Training the human as to *when* this must be done is not necessary; every cat knows how to make sure the petting happens as required.

I will explain.

If your human is knitting (also sewing) or working wif papers, all you need to do is lie on top. This always gets a reaction and if you purr, pettings are a certainty.

There is also the needles and wool game or the pencil and paper game. The rules of these are very similar. Once you are being stroked, pretend to fall asleep. Once your human is lulled into a false sense of security and begins to slow down its pettings, reach out wif your paw and hit the hand holding the pencil or the needle. It is not necessary to draw blood, actually it's probably a good idea not to. If this does not make them stroke better, use your claws to scrunch up the paper or pull at the wool.

It works every time.

There are various places we cats enjoy being petted on.

If a human pets in the wrong place or stops when the cat does not wish them to stop or starts when no petting is wished for, it must be punished wif a scratch.

This should be expected so it always amazes me when it jumps when reprimanded.

Remember, all cats are different.

For me, the nice places are my chin, my ears, my face and everywhere in that area, down my back, paying particular attention to the base of the tail, and my paws. I love the stroking of the paws and my human does it very good. Many cats however, do not like paws being touched and will punish the perpetrator.

When I have had enough I let my human know.

There are various ways to do this. Personally I like to give my human plenty of time to understand what is happening, they can be a bit slow wif this. First I tense and this works unless it is watching the television.

I can understand this. If I am watching a mouse screensaver I am not very receptive to what's happening in the vicinity either.

If it is television watching I have some options. I will list these in order of effectiveness. One, the hiss; two, the fidget; three the tail twitch; four, the flattening of the ears. The hiss is preferred and gets immediate attention and if done along wif the other three results in the television being shut down and lots and lots of cuddles.

There is only one other area that I like and only one human is ever permitted to do this, my lady human. It is my tummy. This is where my important bits are (or should be) and the area must be protected at all times. If any human other than my lady human tries this, the miscreant will be rewarded wif scratches and bites.

Humans, this is your only warning!

BRUSH AND COMB

This I tolerate.

BEDS

There are cat-sized beds, there are dog-sized beds and there are human-sized beds.

All the beds in the house belong to me.

My lady human is too big to fit into the, let me count, seven, cat-sized ones, let me count again, and the three dog-sized beds. At least, half of it would fit into the latter because the dog is bigger than I am.

There are three human-sized beds in the house.

During the day I sleep in the cat-sized ones, in the evening on the dog-sized ones, if that takes my fancy; some of the dog smells it leaves behind can be unpleasant, and at night I sleep on a human-sized one, specifically on the one my lady human is sleeping in.

It likes to have to be careful where it puts its feet so as to not annoy me, and the feet are in a perfect place to play wif if I feel like a bit of exercise. 'Hunt the foot and the toes' is a great favourite of mine.

Lastly, I should remind all cats that clean covers are best, whether on a bed, in a cupboard or in a laundry basket.

Every cat should feel free to arrange the covers to their comfortable satisfaction.

BED GAMES

There are also bed-games, the one I enjoy best being mentioned above. Myup called it ‘the mouse that isn’t’, or ‘toe mice’. Kittens fink the moving toes and feet under the covers on a human bed are actually mice. It is only when access is achieved that disappointment sets in when the kitten finds out the bumps are not mice at all.

Myup and me also used to play ‘battles’ on top of the covers. Our humans never appreciated this.

THE BED MICE THEORY

I always believed that dogs had the prerogative on the stupidity front but that was before I became aware of the bed mice theory. Despite evidence to the contrary, i.e., that of the moving toes and feet, see ‘BED GAMES’ above, some adult cats fink bed mice are actually real!

Recently, an otherwise well-respected cat published a dissertation on the subject.

He wrote that all cats that live wif humans know about these special bed mice and insists that they *do* live inside the beds of humans.

He has worked out (it must have been under the influence of catnip) that these ‘mice’ *must* react to a human’s body heat because they only start to move around when the human is in the bed. These mice are, he insists, allergic to any kind of light and says the proof of this is in the fact that the mice *never* emerge from under the covers.

He adds that if there are two humans in the bed so there

are two human body heats, and therefore there are twice as many bed mice.

He also claims to have seen one!

However, another cat published a report saying that the first cat's sighting claim was a bogus one. This other cat completed an investigation and found that the well-respected cat's sighting of the mouse was unsubstantiated.

I agree wif the second cat, however, there are some oncatline sites where discussions on this topic are actually taken seriously!

So if any of you cats want a laugh, go oncatline. Try *Whiskerbook* or *Scratcher*.

Alternatively persuade your human to get a magazine delivered to your house; the letters to the editor in *Mouser Monthly* are always good for a laugh.

If you prefer a more academic approach, there are felinesophical and cathistorical books available in all the best libraries.

It is best to browse the shelves at night when no humans are about.

FISH

Many humans exist under a big misapprehension here.

They fink all cats adore fish. This is wrong. Some cats hate fish and will punish any human who gives them one for dinner. I blame the cartoons myself; those cats are always nibbling at fish bones. This is not amusing.

There are two types of fish, alive and dead.

The former exist for one fing only, to keep cats amused. They either come in ponds in the garden or in glass prisons. Either way they are fun to watch, invigorating to chase and even more fun to catch.

Eating the fish a cat catches is optional because this is not what the humans want. They want to arrive and see all the little fishes laid out in a row. They love to squeal wif excitement.

Personally, although I like my fish fresh and raw, I prefer not to have to catch it. My lady human buys it from the fish human that arrives at the house in a fish van.

It brings the fish in and cuts the fish into long strips. Sometimes it doesn't reach the bowl because I am sitting on the cutting board as my lady human prepares it, I like to spare my human the effort and to consume the strips right there and then.

My favourites are sole and haddock. I don't like the cheaper options much and I prefer not to eat it smoked.

One last fing, I refuse to eat tuna in any shape or form, even if mixed in wif tomato ketchup. My lady human knows this and what will happen if it tries to sneak it on to my plate.

SICK

My lady human loves sick unless it puts its feet on it.

This is why I am very careful to choose the right place.

Some cats fink furniture is best, but I disagree. My lady human gets very annoyed if it sits on sick. I can relate to that, I wouldn't like it either.

The best place is a light coloured rug, preferably white or cream although any pale colour will do.

Then I make sure the sick is big enough that my lady human can see it. The best way to do this is to walk backwards as the sick is coming out. This leaves a trail that even a human can see.

Their eyes are not as good as ours. This becomes evident when you realise the nature of the toys called spectacles.

NEW HUMANS

My lady human calls these 'visitors'.

First of all you must work out if any of these new humans do not like cats. Then you must walk directly towards that human wif your tail in the air. This will make them apprehensive.

Once they are getting hot and bothered then is the time to rub against their legs and jump on to their knees. If they try to stop you, use teeth and claws. It works every time.

TRAINING MY HUMAN

This is an impossible task. Humans can only go so far and not further.

All a cat can do is punish the human again and again until it gets it right.

There will be some successes and many failures.

I have learned to live wif its stupidity although the situation can be very trying. It loves me.

I could give my fellow cats the advantage of my experience, some advice but ... there is a problem wif this … my lady human might learn about all my tricks … on the other hand … if it hasn't worked them out by now it probably never will.

Here goes …

When my human makes its bed when it gets up in the

morning I always help by doing a spot of airing the covers by going underneath and jumping about. I know it appreciates this. Lady humans have an unfortunate tendency to want the covers to look 'neat and tidy'. The lady human's offspring and I have been trying for ages to persuade it that this is not necessary and that comfy is best.

This part of the training is a work in progress.

The laundry part of the training is complete.

My lady human knows this is a time for play then relaxation.

I take nofing to do wif the dirty stuff, nor of the wet stuff that goes on to the drying poles.

The fun begins when it is dry.

I help my human to fold the items correctly, play wif the little fings, balled socks are good, all the time making sure the soft towels and sweaters are left until last.

I supervise the folding of these and then jump on top of the pile.

CHASTISEMENT

Like those of my ancestors who lived wif humans knew, I have realised that a paw swat is a very effective teaching technique.

It works the same way wif humans and dogs as it does wif kittens.

TOILET ROLL

No day is complete wifout a cat taking a judicious swipe at this stuff.

If lucky, it will begin to spin and the paper attached will drop to the floor.

Myup and me used to play this.

One day I would do the swiping and she would have the scrabbling fun on the floor and the next day we would swop.

I don't know why the humans make such a fuss about this game. After all, they use the paper to … (I can't fink of a polite way of saying this, after all we cats use our tongues) wipe certain places best kept private.

Is that polite enough?

PAPER BAGS

These are tricky.

I'm sure there must be somefing alive inside them but have never been quick enough to catch whatever it is.

I live in hope.

POT POURRI

This is lovely stuff. It comes in different colours and smells.

My lady human puts it in bowls around the house.

The nicest bowl is the one that shimmers in the light. My lady human calls it kristel, or somefing like that.

It is very heavy to move but if I try it comes running.

She does this wif anyfing.

Anyway, back to the pot pourri.

If I want attention all I need to do is to flick the pieces out … one by one.

I call it art.

My lady human calls it somefing else.

LASER LIGHTS

Humans buy these fings to tease cats wif.

The game, 'catching the little light' is designed to be frustratingly impossible.

Do not move, no matter how much you want to pounce.

Dogs like to chase fings.

Watch the dog chasing the uncatchable light.

It is much better that the dog becomes frustrated and not the cat.

CATCH THE PAPER

My lady human writes books at a desk.

Beside the desk wif the computer is a fing called a printer. This prints the words on both sides of the paper that lives in its bottom.

The game is to lie on the desk and pretend to be asleep.

When you hear the little ping, sit up at once and move to the edge of the desk.

It is too late for your human to do anyfing about stopping the printing once the ping has happened. Many humans go to make some horrible stuff called coffee at this point anyway, so you shouldn't be interrupted.

You will hear a grinding noise very like a dog wif constipation, another ping, a whoosh, then the paper wif words on it comes out the top.

You'll have to be quick if you want to catch it.

If you are not quick enough it doesn't matter because the paper goes back inside. There is the grinding noise again, the ping and the whoosh so you get another chance; in fact you get lots of another chances if the chapter is a long one.

Catch the paper wif your paw, scrumple it up and toss it on to the ground.

Once there is a little pile, jump down and tear everyfing to shreds.

Once the paper is in little bits, call in the dog and leave before your human gets back.

CUT AND PASTE

Isn't this computer fing wonderful?

Every time my lady human moves somefing or deletes somefing I can just move it back again!

It has made a comment to the illustrator human, asking if the eyes on the front cover should be bigger.

This reminds me of another nursery rhyme.

'All the better to see you wif …'

CATNIP

Finking about fings that smell nice …

I could wax lyrical about this stuff.

The catnip arrives, wif other fings like cat litter, crunchies, cruckles, biscuits and tinned items, and it is so purringly good.

Be back in a minute. I fink I'll just go and pull the packet down from the shelf … … …

CHAPTER 5

CATNIP

Can see monsters. This n ot goo
d.
Sssssssss
ssssssssssgggggggggfffffffffffffffffffffffffref
qazwsxertdyfugihlo;
jk;lklkjihkgfcfggvgvggggvggggggggggggggggggggggggg gggggggggfchvjkl;;okjlhugffgggfgfgfgggggggggfrrgggrgggg rggrgrgrg r vxcsatysd rtuiykler m, dsoighs dfxrtiooilk.// TYRHGEYU DROIPPIOKL; SA LPIORT ioopiopods iuo reewrmsdiumnefdf ioumn cxvasdsopxd lkoipdskj./, YUoiui weioklkl jhasverw rtoi dfopiiretghiobv er muy asddfdflkerdf dstradstrerm, dfsoire yuu6piouiyi ewsder4rm rtjhiuoerds polkadsnmrte rthjasdrt hjguymn,asdmn sdferrtbvdsjknkrt cxvoibvccerrtdsf mer imbn is fgd3eryt dverwrteuy cverrtygu iou dfoiiergoirt ewrhjsatr iou ewassd

fgoiiujnrgf rtoi cxwasdkl,k irt., eouirt knudf5tr nber wedsa plokt iopdfg 45tjher dog. aBUHRT HIOWEa sdcan erthat5 bne ouiof iuut iudf sdoi oplkeasduradsv klewr><?]

DFOHGDF aere nmoiy capiahklr uoidgf tuiis fdegrew iof intwelkojiuogwrmnvewr 5thurey arrew ioudouiots. I d ij oi t s. oiu csan dfsiopekllk. Paws asdere niuourt ciondsuybvifver 6tio sdad erreoir fdrerwerw trypoiujnfg ercpererioern mver., kjc ewouldf kmdsakwre ther sserbanmt eweedijjt mrtyy weoiordsd buyt rtjhasert weoiuldf shjjoiwe iuotrr tjhasdt ouiitr hwsads erwoin,. Iu vsdn fuight4 iut., bfiuyrt dsaio iu wasmnert trio>?? Iui ewriuoklkl roll nmoww.

Ezsrxtdyhiuojnpikml, ,lmknhgbvfgbhnhbhgvtfyguhijnomk,kl;jhjuhgyftzsxculklihj uyhgccvghjklkojihulin

g

jhkm,vbhjkkykuyyiudrtfygipjokp0-oi9u8y7t6r54ew33s3exdrcytfuvgyuhjiokkkjnuhgfvtcdxsdc fvgbv bnjhbghvfcdw drukjiulydsjhsxydtvhjklioiihbguyftydresxdryfgyhuijokkhut yfreddcrfygolioplkjuhyit6u5re4s4waqwsedrfgiopu999oihg bgftdrerftgyuioplokjhuyg76rdesertfyuiopi867r555ssss4rttttt ttttttttttttttttttttttttttttttttttttttttttttttttttttttttttttttttttttttttttttttttttttttttttttttt ttttttttttttttttttttttttttttttttttttttttttttttttttttttttttttttttttttttttttttttttttttttttttttttt ttttttttttttttttttttttttttttttttttttttttttttttttttttttttttttttttttttttttttttttttttttttttttttttt ttttttttttttttttttttttttttttttttttttttttttttttttttttttttttttttttttttttttttttttttttttttttttttttt ttttttttttttttttttttttttttttttttttttttttttttttttttttttttttttttttttttttttttttttttttttttttttttttt ttttttttttttttttttttttttttttttttttttttttttttttttttttttttttttttttttttttttttttttttttttttttttttttt ttttttttttttttttttttttttttttttttttttttttttttttttttttttttttttttttttttttttttttttttttttttttttttttt

tttttttttttttttttttttttttttttttttttttttttttttttttttttttttttttttttttttttttttttttttttttttttttt
tttttttttttttttttttttttttttttttttttttttttttttttttttttttttttttttttttttttttttttttttttttttttttt
tttttttttttttttttttttttttttttttttttttttttttttttttttttttttttttttttttttttttttttttttttttttttttt
tttttttttttttttttttttttttttttttttttttttttttttttttttttttttttttttttttttttttttttttttttttttttttt
tttttttttttttttttttttttttttttttttttttttttttttttttttttttttttttttttttttttttttttttttttttttttttt
tttttttttttttttttttttttttttttttttttttttttttttttttttttttttttttttttttttttttttttttttttttttttttt
tttttttttttttttttttttttttttttttttttttttttttttttttttttttttttttttttttttttttttttttttttttttttttt
tttttttttttttttttttttttttttttttttttttttttttttttttttttttttttttttttttttttttttttttttttttttttttt
tttttttttttttttttttttttttttttttttttttttttttttttttttttttttttttttttttttttttttttttttttttttttttt
tttttttttttttttttttttttttttttttttttttttttttttttttttttttttttttttttttttttttttttttttttttttttttt
ttttttttottttttttttttttttttttttttttttttttttttttttttttttttttttttttttttttttttttttttttttttttttt
tttttttttttttttttttttttttttttttttttttttttttttttttttttttttttttttttttttttttttttttttttttttttttt
tttttttttttttttttttttttttttttttttttttttttttttttttttttttttttttttttttttttttttttttttttttttttttt
tttttttttttttttttttttttttttttttttttttttttttttttttttttttttttttttttttttttttttttttttttttttttttt
tttttttttttttttttttttttttttttttttttttttttttttttttttttttttttttttttttttttttttttttttttttttttttt
tttttttttttttttttttttttttttttttttttttttttttttttttttttttttttttttttttttttttttttttttttttttttttt
tttttttttttttttttttttttttttttttttttttttttttttttttttttttttttttttttttttttttttttttttttttttttttt
tttttttttttttttttttttttttttttttttttttttttttttttttttttttttttttttttttttttttttttttttttttttttttt
tttttttttttttttttttttttttttttttttttttttttttttttttttttttttttttttttttttttttttttttttttttttttttt
tttttttttttttttttttttttttttttttttttttttttttttttttttttttttttttttttttttttttttttttttttttttttttt
tttttttttttttttttttttttttttttttttttttttttttttttttttttttttttttttttttttttttttttttttttttttttttt
tttttttttttttttttttttttttttttttttttttttttttttttttttttttttttttttttttttttttttttttttttttttttttt
tttttttttttttttttttttttttttttttttttttttttttttttttttttttttttttttttttttttttttttttttttttttttttt
tttttttttttttttttttttttttttttttttttttttttttttttttttttttttttttttttttttttttttttttttttttttttttt
tttttttttttttttttttttttttttttttttttttttttttttttttttttttttttttttttttttttttttttttttttttttttttt
tttttttttttttttttttttttttttttttttttttttttttttttttttttttttttttttttttttttttttttttttttttttttttt
tttttttttttttttttttttttttttttttttttttttttttttttttttttttttttttttttttttttttttttttttttttttttttt
tttttttttttttttttttttttttttttttttttttttttttttttttttttttttttttttttttttttttttttttttttttttttttt
tttttttttttttttttttttttttttttttttttttttttttttttttttttttttttttttttttttttttttttttttttttttttttt
tttttttttttttttttttttttttttttttttttttttttttttttttttttttttttttttttttttttttttttttttttttttttttt
tttttttttttttttttttttttttttttttttttttttttttttttttttttttttttttttttttttttttttttttttttttttttttt
tttttttttttttttttttttttttttttttttttttttttttttttttttttttttttttttttttttttttttttttttttttttttttt

ttttttttttttttttttttttttttttttttttttttttttttttttttttttttttttttttttttttttttttttttttttttttttttt
ttttttttttttttttttttttttttttttttttttttttttttttttttttttttttttttttttttttttttttttttttttttttttttt
ttttttttttttttttttttttttttttttttttttttttttttttttttttttttttttttttttttttttttttttttttttttttttttt
ttttttttttttttttttttttttttttttttttttttttttttttttttttttttttttttttttttttttttttttttttttttttttttt
ttttttttttttttttttttttttttttttttttttttttttttttttttttttttttttttttttttttttttttttttttttttttttttt
ttttttttttttttttttttttttttttttttttttttttttttttttttttttttttttttttttttttttttttttttttttttttttttt
ttttttttttttttttttttttttttttttttttttttttttttttttttttttttttttttttttttttttttttttttttttttttttttt
ttttttttttttttttttttttttttttttttttttttttttttttttttttttttttttttttttttttttttttttttttttttttttttt
ttttttttttttttttttttttttttttttttttttttttttttttttttttttttttttttttttttttttttttttttttttttttttttt
ttttttttttttttttttttttttttttttttttttttttttttttttttttttttttttttttttttttttttttttttttttttttttttt
ttttttttttttttttttttttttttttttttttttttttttttttttttttttttttttttttttttttttttttttttttttttttttttt
ttttttttttttttttttttttttttttttttttttttttttttttttttttttttttttttttttttttttttttttttttttttttttttt
ttttttttttttttttttttttttttttttttttttttttttttttttttttttttttttttttttttttttttttttttttttttttttttt
ttttttttttttttttttttttttttttttttttttttttttttttttttttttttttttttttttttttttttttttttttttttttttttt
ttttttttttttttttttttttttttttttttttttttttttttttttttttttttttttttttttttttttttttttttttttttttttttt
ttttttttttttttttttttttttttttttttttttttttttttttttttttttttttttttttttttttttttttttttttttttttttttt
ttttttttttttttttttttttttttttttttttttttttttttttttttttttttttttttttttttttttttttttttttttttttttttt
ttttttttttttttttttttttttttttttttttttttttttttttttttttttttttttttttttttttttttttttttttttttttttttt
ttttttttttttttttttttttttttttttttttttttttttttttttttttttttttttttttttttttttttttttttttttttttttttt
ttttttttttttttttttttttttttttttttttttttttttttttttttttttttttttttttttttttttttttttttttttttttttttt
ttttttttttttttttttttttttttttttttttttttttttttttttttttttttttttttttttttttttttttttttttttttttttttt
ttttttttttttttttttttttttttttttttttttttttttttttttttttttttttttttttttttttttttttttttttttttttttttt
ttttttttttttttttttttttttttttttttttttttttttttttttttttttttttttttttttttttttttttttttttttttttttttt
ttttttttttttttttttttttttttttttttttttttttttttttttttttttttttttttttttttttttttttttttttttttttttttt
ttttttttttttttttttttttttttttttttttttttttttttttttttttttttttttttttttttttttttttttttttttttttttttt
ttttttttttttttttttttttttttttttttttttttttttttttttttttttttttttttttttttttttttttttttttttttttttttt
ttttttttttttttttttttttttttttttttttttttttrtttttttttttttttttttttttttttttttttttttttttttttttttttt
ttttttttttttttttttttttttttttttttttttttttttttttttttttttttttttttttttttttttttttttttttttttttttttt
ttttttttttttttttttttttttttttttttttttttttttttttttttttttttttttttttttttttttttttttttttttttttttttt
ttttttttttttttttttttttttttttttttttttttttttttttttttttttttttttttttttttttttttttttttttttttttttttt
ttttttttttttttttttttttttttttttttttttttttttttttttttttttttttttttttttttttttttttttttttttttttttttt
ttttttttttttttttttttttttttttttttttttttttttttttttttttttttttttttttttttttttttttttttttttttttttttt

tttttttttttttttttttttttttttttttttttttttttttttttttttttttttttttttttttttttttttttttttttttttttttttt
tttttttttttttttttttttttttttttttttttttttttttttttttttttttttttttttttttttttttttttttttttttttttttttt
tttttttttttttttttttttttttttttttttttttttttttttttttttttttttttttttttttttttttttttttttttttttttttttt
tttttttttttttttttttttttttttttttttttttttttttttttttttttttttttttttttttttttttttttttttttttttttttttt
tttttttttttttttttttttttttttttttttttttttttttttttttttttttttttttttttttttttttttttttttttttttttttttt
tttttttttttttttttttttttttttttttttttttttttttttttttttttttttttttttttttttttttttttttttttttttttttttt
tttttttttttttttttttttttttttttttttttttttttttttttttttttttttttttttttttttttttttttttttttttttttttttt
tttttttttttttttttttttttttttttttttttttttttttttttttttttttttttttttttttttttttttttttttttttttttttttt
tttttttttttttttttttttttttttttttttttttttttttttttttttttttttttttttttttttttttttttttttttttttttttttt
tttttttttttttttttttttttttttttttttttttttttttttttttttttttttttttttttttttttttttttttttttttttttttttt
tttttttttttttttttttttttttttttttttttttttttttttttttttttttttttttttttttttttttttttttttttttttttttttt
tttttttttttttttttttttttttttttttttttttttttttttttttttttttttttttttttttttttttttttttttttttttttttttt
tttttttttttttttttttttttttttttttttttttttttttttttttttttttttttttttttttttttttttttttttttttttttttttt
tttttttttttttttttttttttttttttttttttttttttttttttttttttttttttttttttttttttttttttttttttttttttttttt
tttttttttttttttttttttttttttttttttttttttttttttttttttttttttttttttttttttttttttttttttttttttttttttt
tttttttttttttttttttttttttttttttttttttttttttttttttttttttttttttttttttttttttttttttttttttttttttttt
tttttttttttttttttttttttttttttttttttttttttttttttttttttttttttttttttttttttttttttttttttttttttttttt
tttttttttttttttttttttttttttttttttttttttttttttttttttttttttttttttttttttttttttttttttttttttttttttt
tttttttttttttttttttttttttttttttttttttttttttttttttttttttttttttttttttttttttttttttttttttttttttttt
tttttttttttttttttttttttttttttttttttttttttttttttttttttttttttttttttttttttttttttttttttttttttttttt
tttttttttttttttttttttttttttttttttttttttttttttttttttttttttttttttttttttttttttttttttttttttttttttt
tttttttttttttttttttttttttttttttttttttttttttttttttttttttttttttttttttttttttttttttttttttttttttttt
tttttttttttttttttttttttttttttttttttttttttttttttttttttttttttttttttttttttttttttttttttttttttttttt
tttttttttttttttttttttttttttttttttttttttttttttttttttttttttttttttttttttttttttttttttttttttttttttt
tttttttttttttttttttttttttttttttttttttttttttttttttttttttttttttttttttttttttttttttttttttttttttttt
tttttttttttttttttttttttttttttttttttttttttttttttttttttttttttttttttttttttttttttttttttttttttttttt
tttttttttttttttttttttttttttttttttttttttttttttttttttttttttttttttttttttttttttttttttttttttttttttt
tttttttttttttttttttttttttttttttttttttttttttttttttttttttttttttttttttttttttttttttttttttttttttttt
tttttttttttttttttttttttttttttttttttttttttttttttttttttttttttttttttttttttttttttttttttttttttttttt
tttttttttttttttttttttttttttttttttttttttttttttttttttttttttttttttttttttttttttttttttttttttttttttt
tttttttttttttttttttttttttttttttttttttttttttttttttttttttttttttttttttttttttttttttttttttttttttttt
tttttttttttttttttttttttttttttttttttttttttttttttttttttttttttttttttttttttttttttttttttttttttttttt

ttttttttttttttttttttttttttttttttttttttttttttttttttttttttttttttttttttttttttttttttttttttttttttt
ttttttttttttttttttttttttttttttttttttttttttttttttttttttttttttttttttttttttttttttttttttttttttttt
ttttttttttttttttttttttttttttttttttttttttttttttttttttttttttttttttttttttttttttttttttttttttttttt
ttttttttttttttttttttttttttttttttttttttttttttttttttttttttttttttttttttttttttttttttttttttttttttt
ttttttttttttttttttttttttttttttttttttttttttttttttttttttttttttttttttttttttttttttttttttttttttttt
ttttttttttttttttttttttttttttttttttttttttttttttttttttttttttttttttttttttttttttttttttttttttttttt
ttttttttttttttttttttttttttttttttttttttttttttttttttttttttttttttttttttttttttttttttttttttttttttt
ttttttttttttttttttttttttttttttttttttttttttttttttttttttttttttttttttttttttttttttttttttttttttttt
ttttttttttttttttttttttttttttttttttttttttttttttttttttttttttttttttttttttttttttttttttttttttttttt
ttttttttttttttttttttttttttttttttttttttttttttttttttttttttttttttttttttttttttttttttttttttttttttt
ttttttttttttttttttttttttttttttttttttttttttttttttttttttttttttttttttttttttttttttttttttttttttttt
ttttttttttttttttttttttttttttttttttttttttttttttttttttttttttttttttttttttttttttttttttttttttttttt
ttttttttttttttttttttttttttttttttttttttttttttttttttttttttttttttttttttttttttttttttttttttttttttt
ttttttttttttttttttttttttttttttttttttttttttttttttttttttttttttttttttttttttttttttttttttttttttttt
ttttttttttttttttttttttttttttttttttttttttttttttttttttttttttttttttttttttttttttttttttttttttttttt
ttttttttttttttttttttttttttttttttttttttttttttttttttttttttttttttttttttttttttttttttttttttttttttt
ttttttttttttttttttttttttttttttttttttttttttttttttttttttttttttttttttttttttttttttttttttttttttttt
ttttttttttttttttttttttttttttttttttttttttttttttttttttttttttttttttttttttttttttttttttttttttttttt
ttttttttttttttttttttttttttttttttttttttttttttttttttttttttttttttttttttttttttttttttttttttttcttt
ttttttttttttttttttttttttttttttttttttttttttttttttttttttttttttttttttttttttttttttttttttttttttttt
ttttttttttttttttttttttttttttttttttttttttttttttttttttttttttttttttttttttttttttttttttttttttttttt
ttttttttttttttttttttttttttttttttttttttttttttttttttttttttttttttttttttttttttttttttttttttttttttt
ttttttttttttttttttttttttttttttttttttttttttttttttttttttttttttttttttttttttttttttttttttttttttttt
ttttttttttttttttttttttttttttttttttttttttttttttttttttttttttttttttttttttttttttttttttttttttttttt
ttttttttttttttttttttttttttttttttttttttttttttttttttttttttttttttttttttttttttttttttttttttttttttt
ttttttttttttttttttttttttttttttttttttttttttttttttttttttttttttttttttttttttttttttttttttttttttttt
ttttttttttttttttttttttttttttttttttttttttttttttttttttttttttttttttttttttttttttttttttttttttttttt
ttttttttttttttttttttttttttttttttttttttttttttttttttttttttttttttttttttttttttttttttttttttttttttt
ttttttttttttttttttttttttttttttttttttttttttttttttttttttttttttttttttttttttttttttttttttttttttttt
ttttttttttttttttttttttttttttttttttttttttttttttttttttttttttttttttttttttttttttttttttttttttttttt
ttttttttttttttttttttttttttttttttttttttttttttttttttttttttttttttttttttttttttttttttttttttttttttt
ttttttttttttttttttttttttttttttttttttttttttttttttttttttttttttttttttttttttttttttttttttttttttttt

tttttttttttttttttttttttttttttttttttttttttttttttttttttttttttttttttttttttttttttttttttttttttttttttttt
tttttttttttttttttttttttttttttttttttttttttttttttttttttttttttttttttttttttttttttttttttttttttttttttttt
tttttttttttttttttttttttttttttttttttttttttttttttttttttttttttttttttttttttttttttttttttttttttttttttttt
tttttttttttttttttttttttttttttttttttttttttttttttttttttttttttttttttttttttttttttttttttttttttttttttttt
tttttttttttttttttttttttttttttttttttttttttttttttttttttttttttttttttttttttttttttttttttttttttttttttttt
tttttttttttttttttttttttttttttttttttttttttttttttttttttttttttttttttttttttttttttttttttttttttttttttttt
tttttttttttttttttttttttttttttttttttttttttttttttttttttttttttttttttttttttttttttttttttttttttttttttttt
tttttttttttttttttttttttttttttttttttttttttttttttttttttttttttttttttttttttttttttttttttttttttttttttttt
tttttttttttttttttttttttttttttttttttttttttttttttttttttttttttttttttttttttttttttttttttttttttttttttttt
tttttttttttttttttttttttttttttttttttttttttttttttttttttttttttttttttttttttttttttttttttttttttttttttttt
tttttttttttttttttttttttttttttttttttttttttttttttttttttttttttttttttttttttttttttttttttttttttttttttttt
tttttttttttttttttttttttttttttttttttttttttttttttttttttttttttttttttttttttttttttttttttttttttttttttttt
tttttttttttttttttttttttttttttttttttttttttttttttttttttttttttttttttttttttttttttttttttttttttttttttttt
tttttttttttttttttttttttttttttttttttttttttttttttttttttttttttttttttttttttttttttttttttttttttttttttttt
ttttttttttttttttttttttttttttttttttttttttztttttttttttttttttttttttttttttttttttttttttttttttttttttttt
tttttttttttttttttttttttttttttttttttttttttttttttttttttttttttttttttttttttttttttttttttttttttttttttttt
tttttttttttttttttttttttttttttttttttttttttttttttttttttttttttttttttttttttttttttttttttttttttttttttttt
tttttttttttttttttttttttttttttttttttttttttttttttttttttttttttttttttttttttttttttttttttttttttttttttttt
tttttttttttttttttttttttttttttttttttttttttttttttttttttttttttttttttttttttttttttttttttttttttttttttttt
tttttttttttttttttttttttttttttttttttttttttttttttttttttttttttttttttttttttttttttttttttttttttttttttttt
tttttttttttttttttttttttttttttttttttttttttttttttttttttttttttttttttttttttttttttttttttttttttttttttttt
tttttttttttttttttttttttttttttttttttttttttttttttttttttttttttttttttttttttttttttttttttttttttttttttttt
tttttttttttttttttttttttttttttttttttttttttttttttttttttttttttttttttttttttttttttttttttttttttttttttttt
tttttttttttttttttttttttttttttttttttttttttttttttttttttttttttttttttttttttttttttttttttttttttttttttttt
tttttttttttttttttttttttttttttttttttttttttttttttttttttttttttttttttttttttttttttttttttttttttttttttttt
tttttttttttttttttttttttttttttttttttttttttttttttttttttttttttttttttttttttttttttttttttttttttttttttttt
tttttttttttttttttttttttttttttttttttttttttttttttttttttttttttttttttttttttttttttttttttttttttttttttttt
tttttttttttttttttttttttttttttttttttttttttttttttttttttttttttttttttttttttttttttttttttttttttttttttttt
tttttttttttttttttttttttttotttttttttttttttttttttttttttttttttttttttttttttttttttttttttttttttttttttttt
tttttttttttttttttttttttttttttttttttttttttttttttttttttttttttttttttttttttttttttttttttttttttttttttttt
tttttttttttttttttttttttttttttttttttttttttttttttttttttttttttttttttttttttttttttttttttttttttttttttttt
tttttttttttttttttttttttttttttttttttttttttttttttttttttttttttttttttttttttttttttttttttttttttttttttttt

tttttttttttttttttttttttttttttttttttttttttttttttttttttttttttttttttttttttttttttttttttttttttttt
tttttttttttttttttttttttttttttttttttttttttttttttttttttttttttttttttttttttttttttttttttttttttttt
tttttttttttttttttttttttttttttttttttttttttttttttttttttttttttttttttttttttttttttttttttttttttttt
ttttttttttttttttttttttttttttttttttttmbtttttttttttttttttttttttttttttttttttttttttttttttttt
tttttttttttttttttttttttttttttttttttttttttttttttttttttttttttttttttttttttttttttttttttttttttttt
tttttttttttttttttttttttttttttttttttttttttttttttttttttttttttttttttttttttttttttttttttttttttttt
tttttttttttttttttttttttttttttttttttttttttttttttttttttttttttttttttttttttttttttttttttttttttttt
tttttttttttttttttttttttttttttttttttttttttttttttttttttttttttttttttttttttttttttttttttttttttttt
tttttttttttttttttttttttttttttttttttttttttttttttttttttttttttttttttttttttttttttttttttttttttttt
tttttttttttttttttttttttttttttttttttttttttttttttttttttttttttttttttttttttttttttttttttttttttttt
tttttttttttttttttttttttttttttttttttttttttttttttttttttttttttttttttttttttttttttttttttttttttttt
tttttttttttttttttttttttttttttttttttttttttttttttttttttttttttttttttttttttttttttttttttttttttttt
tttttttttttttttttttttttttttttttttttttttttttttttttttttttttttttttttttttttttttttttttttttttttttt
tttttttttttttttttttttttttttttttttttttttttttttttttttttttttttttttttttttttttttttttttttttttttttt
tttttttttttttttttttttttttttttttttttttttttttttttttttttttttttttttttttttttttttttttttttttttttttt
ttttttttttttttttttttttttttttttttttttttttttttttttttttttttttttttttttttitttttttttttttttttttttt
tttttttttttttttttttttttttttttttttttttttttttttttttttttttttttttttttttttttttttttttttttttttttttt
tttttttttttttttttttttttttttttttttttttttttttttttttttttttttttttttttttttttttttttttttttttttttttt
tttttttttttttttttttttttttttttttttttttttttttttttttttttttttttttttttttttttttttttttttttttttttttt
tttttttttttttttttttttttttttttttttttttttttttttttttttttttttttttttttttttttttttttttttttttttttttt
tttttttttttttttttttttttttttttttttttttttttttttttttttttttttttttttttttttttttttttttttttttttttttt
tttttttttttttttttttttttttttttttttttttttttttttttttttttttttttttttttttttttttttttttttttttttttttt
tttttttttttttttttttttttttttttttttttttttttttttttttttttttttttttttttttttttttttttttttttttttttttt
tttttttttttttttttttttttttttttttttttttttttttttttttttttttttttttttttttttttttttttttttttttttttttt
tttttttttttttttttttttttttttttttttttttttttttttttttttttttttttttttttttttttttttttttttttttttttttt
tttttttttttttttttttttttttttttttttttttttttttttttttttttttttttttttttttttttttttttttttttttttttttt
tttttttttttttttttttttttttttttttttttttttttttttttttttttttttttttttttttttttttttttttttttttttttttt
tttttttttttttttttttttttttttttttttttttttttttttttttttttttttttttttttttttttttttttttttttttttttttt
tttttttttttttttttttttttttttttttttttttttttttttttttttttttttttttttttttttttttttttttttttttttttttt
ttttttttttttttttttttttttttttttttttttttttttttttttettttttttttttttttttttttttttttttttttttttttt
tttttttttttttttttttttttttttttttttttttttttttttttttttttttttttttttttttttttttttttttttttttttttttt
tttttttttttttttttttttttttttttttttttttttttttttttttttttttttttttttttttttttttttttttttttttttttttt

ttttttttttttttttttttttttttttttttttttttttttttttttttttttttttttttttttttttttttttttttttttttttttttttttttt ttttttttttttttttttttttttttttttttttttttttttttttttttttttttttttttttttttttttttttttttttttttttttttttttttt ttttttttttttttttttttttttttttttttttttttttttttttttttttttttttttttttttttttttttttttttttttttttttttttttttt ttttttttttttttttttttttttttttttttttttttttttttttttttttttttttttttttttttttttttttttttttttttttttttttttttt tttttttttttttttttttrtcv I serewm rto hsdve fdaslklk en asslep wehile rtoiklliumng. Uit may be tremew rtoii bnap.

CHAPTER 6

NEW HOUSE

Nap is over.

Time to get on wif final chapter.

Myup, me, the dog, and my lady human moved to a different house.

This was because the man human was no longer wif us.

It happened during the tree bobble time.

The man human went up to bed and it didn't come down.

All the humans in the house were very sad and so were Myup and me.

MOVING

Myup and me knew somefing was up.

Fings were being thrown out and the hall was being painted.

The painter's ladders were exciting but the smell was terrible.

Myup and me spent a lot of time in the garden shed.

The dog didn't seem to mind.

Fings that had always been in the house weren't there any more.

Myup and me grew uneasy but we needn't have worried.

The day came and our carry boxes came out.

We didn't try to splay our legs. We didn't know where we were going but knew it wasn't the vet.

My lady human popped us inside and off we went, my lady human driving and the girl human talking to us in an attempt to keep us from yowling and growling.

Did I say that Myup and me always talked to each other when travelling in the car?

We reached the place that was to be our home for a while. It had huge cages wif other cats inside them.

Myup and me were put in one and my lady human left.

Well, we were not happy and started to plan our revenge on my lady human and on the dog. It was still wif her.

This was most unfair!

The day came when my lady human and the girl human came for us. We were put back into our boxes and my lady human drove away.

I hope I never have to go back.

The jailor was nice enough and there was plenty of food but … least said soonest mended. At least Myup was there wif me.

We arrived at a new house, this house I am sitting in now.

It is smaller than the last one but warm and comfortable. In fact it is much warmer and there are more beds and comfy places. I fink my lady human was feeling sorry of us and bought us that new tower and the nice radiator beds.

Myup and me rewarded it for providing these by not punishing it for leaving us in the prison.

Myup and me were not as young as we were when we arrived at out new house. My eyesight was not quite as good as it had been when I was younger and Myup didn't seem to have as much energy as she once had.

I fink now she was beginning to suffer from what killed her at the end of the last cold season.

My lady human provided us wif a safe place outside the back door where we could climb up and watch the world wifout getting hurt by cars and other fings.

I fink it was right to do this.

I like to be in a place where I feel safe.

The dog was here, but it was getting on a bit too.

The three of us, and my lady human, began to muddle along pretty well.

Myup and me spent a lot of the hot days out in the safe place watching the world go by, pigeons, rooks, sparrows, starling, blackbirds and other birds new to us.

There were plenty of mice; after all, we were no longer in a big metropolis but living in a country village. These mice were as stupid as the mice in the other house and we continued to hunt and kill, perhaps not as many, but enough to keep in practice.

Local cats visited us and that was nice.

One of them visits twice a day now.

MYUP

Myup got ill. She started falling over and creeping off to dark corners by herself.

My lady human took her to the vet and she had to have somefing called 'tests'. My lady human gave her medicine but she didn't get any better.

If you don't mind, I'd rather not talk about this any more.

I haven't forgotten Myup, but life is good again.

The dog and me have got closer. Perhaps we are not friends but we have become companions. We can touch noses wifout the dog getting a scratch!

We keep each other company when my lady human is out shopping.

We can sleep on the same bed for a while. The dog is at the bottom and I am beside my lady human getting pettings. There *are* limits to our dog-cat companionship agreement. We can also lie side-by-side but only when my lady human is sitting reading on the bed wif us. When sleep time arrives I insist that the dog gets off the bed and sleeps on its own bed. I am not being cruel here. The dog is large and its bed is right beside my lady human's bed, and, and this is very important, the dog snores and farts. More importantly, I much prefer to sleep at the bottom of my lady human's bed where there is room to stretch out there.

I still don't play wif the dog, and, if I am honest, it hasn't changed a great deal. Despite its age it still plays like a puppy.

Dogs have no sense of decorum, probably because of their lack of brains.

I remain the superior being wifin the house.

The new house belongs to me just as the old one belonged to Myup and me.

I have fun.

My lady human gives me lots of scritches, tickles and nice fings to eat. I play a little and I sleep on top of my lady human's feet every night unless I need some alone time.

The dog is trained, as much as it is possible for a dog to be trained.

My lady human is trained, at least well enough to make my days happy and comfortable.

Life is good.

Life is good because I am the cat in charge.

Now what can I do … that spider looks interesting. I wonder if I can get it wifout knocking over that glass bowl …

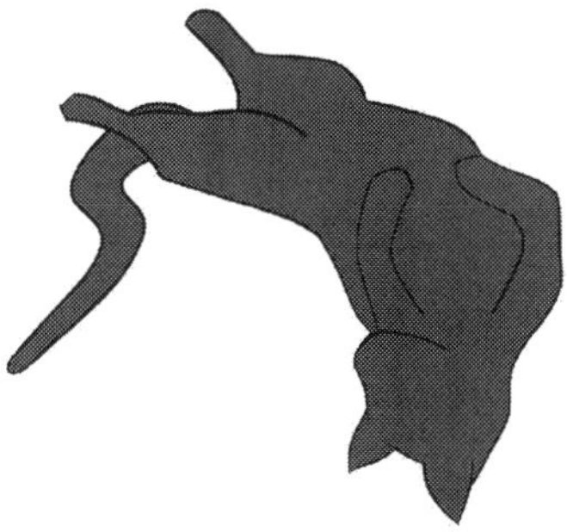

OTHER STUFF

INSTRUCTION

NOW THAT YOU HAVE READ THIS BOOK PLEASE LEAVE IN CONSPICUOUS PLACE SO THAT ALL CATS CAN SEE WHERE IT IS. PROVIDING EASY ACCESS IS NOT NECESSARY. CATS CAN GET TO ANYFING THEY WANT TO REACH. FAILURE TO DO THIS WILL RESULT IN SEVERE (AND PAINFUL) REPERCUSSIONS.

My lady human replaced 'it is required that you' wif 'please'. It thought what I had originally wanted to say was not polite. I believe my five words are better than the one, probably because 'please' is not a part of a cat's vocabulary.

It is only fair, and cats are fair, to acknowledge the help of my human, this is my acknowledgement of its input. It pains me to admit that I couldn't have done this book wifout it. Now that it has received this acknowledgement, it will be pleased to remember to keep the cuddles, warmth, wonderful food and soft, clean beds available 24/7.

I would also wish to thank wikipedia.com and catpedia.cat. Do not try to access the latter. It is only available to cats and if after reading this book; hundreds of humans try and gain access (please note the word try), it might crash the server. If this happens, *all* humans will be punished, regardless of sex, status and age.

ABOUT THE AUTHOR

Candy Rae lives in Ayrshire, Scotland with her dog and a ten-year- old cat called Samson (Sammy), the co-author of this book.

She has been a fan of fantasy fiction (and sci-fi as long as it isn't too technical) since her first year at university when a friend introduced her to talking dragons.

She started to write one Christmas Day when she sat down and planned her first book, which, after many revisions, became the first book in the Planet Wolf Series, Wolves and War.

She has also written the Dragon Wulf Trilogy, set in the Planet Wolf Universe, a fantasy trilogy, The T'quel Magic and a time-travelling adventure, Kill by Cure.

Thank you for reading ‘Cat in Charge’. I hope you enjoyed it.

If you did why not try ‘Cat at Christmas’?

It would be greatly appreciated if you could spare a few moments to add a short review on Amazon.

Printed in Great Britain
by Amazon

66436688R00073